SNOW BOUND

SNOW

BOUND

HARRY MAZER

DELACORTE PRESS / NEW YORK

Mazer, Harry.
  Snow Bound.

  SUMMARY: Two teenagers caught in a snowstorm face a fight
for survival in a desolate area.
  [1. Survival—Fiction]   I. Title.
PZ7.M47397Sn   [Fic]   72–7958

To Norma,
without whom there would have been no book

AUTHOR'S NOTE

"Without a doubt the most forbidding and
unknown physiographic region in New
York State is the great windswept plateau
called Tug Hill. On a road map it is that
strange blank area of roughly two hundred
thousand acres approximately twenty miles
southeast of Watertown and thirty miles
northwest of Utica. An effort to locate a
hamlet or even a dirt road in this enigmatic
area can only be rewarded with
frustration. . . ."

PAUL WEINMAN
(reprinted from *NAHO*, Fall, 1970
published by the New York State
Museum and Science Service)

CONTENTS

SNOW BOUND

1

TONY

IT WAS the middle of January and the snow was melting. All the way home from school, Tony Laporte, his fringed suede jacket open, packed snowballs, leaving a trail of white-splattered trees behind him. The mark of Tony Laporte.

Everyone was talking about the unseasonably warm weather. "It won't last," his father said. The January thaw would be followed by a drop in temperature, a freeze. There would be a blizzard in February, his father predicted. Even so, that morning, before they'd gone to work, his father had turned down the thermostat, and his mother, already in her brown car coat, had opened the windows and pushed the storms out wide.

Tony packed a huge snowball and looked around

for a suitable target. The warm weather made him itch to do something different. The unchanging routine of school, play, home was driving him batty. For once in his life he wished something would happen. Something real and different. Like that guy stepping off a ladder onto the moon. Now that was something!

This last year Tony had sprung up out of his baby fat, gaining four inches, wide shoulders, body hair, and a chin full of pimples. The pimples worried him. He couldn't help examining them, rubbing them, poking, squeezing. His sister Donna caught him in front of the mirror a couple of times and called him conceited. "That's right," he'd retorted. "Don't you wish you had something as good to look at!"

Tony paused at the edge of Bridge Street, still cradling the snowball. His house was the yellow two-family at the edge of the bridge that spanned a deep ravine through which ran the double tracks of the New York Central Railroad. The landlords, Mr. and Mrs. Bielec, lived downstairs, while Tony's family lived upstairs.

He didn't feel like going into his house yet. It was the same old thing every day: school, home, change your clothes, eat, watch TV, go to bed. Then all over again the next day. Nothing happened in his life; and the way he felt just then, nothing ever would.

He heaved the snowball at a long silver truck rolling slowly across the bridge. The driver raised a fist. Tony strode alongside the truck, grinning at the driver. The driver might have rolled down the window and really blasted him, but what Tony was imagining was

2

the driver pulling over, opening the door on the passenger side, and offering him a ride. The driver would want company to Cleveland or Chicago. Tony could drive on the long, open stretches. Maybe they'd become partners and drive all over the country together.

A horn blast brought him back to reality. He was standing on the edge of the road, daydreaming. Annoyed that he'd been caught, he climbed over the guardrail at the end of the bridge and went sliding down the wet slope. He and his friends had built a clubhouse last summer in a clump of crooked sumac trees on the side of the hill. They had used scrap lumber taken from a building site, odd two-by-fours, and scraps of plywood.

He imagined he heard voices coming from the shack. A family trapped by the snow, waiting for the ski patrol . . . a mother and her kids. They'd been without food or heat, and when he appeared they could hardly speak for tears of happiness . . .

Tony came on the dog by surprise—a large brown mutt with a black muzzle and ropy black tail, lying down near the entrance to their shack, gnawing into a bag of garbage. Sensing Tony, he raised his head, then rose to his feet, hair bristling, muzzle wrinkled.

Tony slowly approached the dog. "Easy, boy . . ."

The dog arched his back like a spring, his forehead crisscrossed with angry wrinkles. He snarled. Tony stood his ground. "Easy, boy. Easy." He felt a slight bristling on his own skin, but no real fear. The dog snapped at his boots. Tony reached down and surprised the dog by whapping it across the muzzle. He was prepared to hit the dog again, but the creature gurgled back a growl and sat down submissively on his haunches.

"Good boy, good dog," Tony said approvingly. The worried brown eyes looked deeply into his. The dog had sense, make no mistake of it. He'd run away from a circus, or . . . perhaps he'd been trained to nose out hidden bombs. Tony saw himself and the dog as a two-member team of bomb experts going briskly and confidently into situations that older men feared . . .

Finding the dog was a good omen, Tony thought. Some impulse had brought him down here to the club-house to discover the dog. It had to mean something. Tony saw the dog as a courier, a messenger that he only had to follow to be led to an important rendezvous.

"Okay, lead me someplace."

The dog watched him, his eyes on Tony's face, waiting.

"You're hungry. Is that right, pooch? Food first, action later." Tony straightened up. "Come on, I'll get you something good to eat." He looked back. The dog was following. "Come on, Arthur. That's a good boy, Arthur." He'd name him King Arthur, after the pop singer. The dog knew his name at once! It was all part of the strange but natural way he had come into Tony's life. Almost as if the dog had been sent to be his.

As Tony and Arthur started home, there was a chill in the air, and puddles of water were crusting with thin ice. Tony looked up at his own house, to the warmth behind the yellow windows on the second floor. His three sisters were probably at home.

4

Later when his father pulled into the driveway, Tony was out front waiting to show him the dog. At the sight of Mr. Laporte, the dog started to bark, snarling and backing away. "It's okay, Arthur. It's okay," Tony soothed. "That's my father. He's okay—a friend." He scratched the dog under the ear, and the animal sat down.

"Thanks for the endorsement," Fred Laporte said. He was only half a head taller than his son, but stockier, with a round red face and thinning hair. He wore green work pants and a quilted green jacket, unzipped. "What have you got there, a man-eating tiger?"

"His name is King Arthur. I'm going to keep him." Tony talked fast, pointing out all the dog's fine points, his warm brown eyes, his keen sense of smell, the way he responded to directions. "He's really special. We're lucky to have him, Pop!"

"Not so fast," his father said, toeing a scrap of soggy paper from the lawn. "You're not talking me into this the way you did guitar lessons—"

"It's not the same," Tony interrupted. "I didn't care about music that much. It was Mom's idea, not mine."

"I wish you'd thought of it before I put out all that money. Who does this dog belong to? He must belong to somebody."

"That's the point," Tony replied, opening the fingers of his left hand. "No collar, no leash. The dog was hungry. He was looking for someone, and there I was."

"You'll change your mind in five minutes. What

5

about taking care of him? You don't do anything around this place without your arm being twisted. And besides, your mother is afraid of dogs."

"She'll let me keep him," Tony said confidently. He knew his parents through and through. They might say no at first to something he wanted; they might say no if they were mad or tired, but they came around. They always had, and they always would. His parents had often said that they both worked because they wanted their kids to have a better life than they'd had. His father made good money at Turbine and also pulled down extra money as union steward. His mother was a skilled machine operator at Tex-Lite. They'd been the first family on Bridge Street with a color TV set, a Zenith console in a coffee-colored early American cabinet. His father drove a late-model Ford wagon, and his mother had a little Plymouth of her own.

"A family like ours needs a dog," Tony went on.

"Have you forgotten Christmas? It isn't even a month yet," his father said, reminding him of the Ted Williams baseball glove, the suede fringed jacket he was wearing, plus the little Sony TV of his own. "You got plenty of stuff, so don't tell me about a dog. When I was your age I was out of school and working in a fruit market to help out my family."

"Do you want me to go to work?" Tony had heard about how hard his parents had worked and how easy he and his sisters had it more times than he cared to remember. "I'll quit school tomorrow and find a job."

"What am I working my back off for?" his father said. "So you can grow up to be a dummy like your

6

parents? You stay in school and learn to use your brain instead of your back."

"I want this dog," Tony said.

"We'll talk about it."

"You can talk all you want," Tony said, "but I'm keeping King Arthur."

His father reached out and grabbed Tony in his heavy arms. "You're as tough as the old man, aren't you?" he said proudly. "Nobody tells you anything, right?" His father turned him around and gave him a friendly tap on the butt. "But don't forget who the *really* tough guy in this family is."

"No! I don't care if his name is Nelson Rockefeller. I don't want a dog in this house. Dog hairs, dog dirt, dog do. Between you and your sisters I have enough dogs underfoot right now."

Bev Laporte had just come home from work herself. She had kicked off her boots, but was still wearing her tan slacks and short suede jacket as she made supper, running from the sink to the stove to the refrigerator, and yelling at Tony's three sisters, Evie, Donna, and Flo, for leaving the kitchen a mess.

"Why doesn't *he* help?" said Flo, his older sister, pointing a finger at Tony. "Just because he's a boy! He makes a bigger mess than anyone."

"What do I have girls for, to give me arguments?" Mrs. Laporte said. "Get off your fanny and get busy on the salad. Get that dog out from under my feet, Tony. If he rubs against my leg once more I'm going to scream. Did your father say you could keep him?"

"Dad's impressed with this dog. He says he's a fine dog. Only he wants him to be bigger and stronger. You got anything to eat? That's why he's nervous." Tony was tying a piece of string around the dog's neck and winding it loosely around the doorknob. "He wants something good to eat, Mom. What do you have good?"

"Don't you give him anything without asking my permission first," his mother said. "This isn't a dog refugee camp."

Tony went to the refrigerator and took out yesterday's meat loaf. He was scraping off the tomato sauce when his mother saw what he was doing.

"My meat loaf!" she exclaimed. "Put that back. I didn't give you permission. You kids will drive me crazy. That's for your father's sandwiches tomorrow."

"There's salami and capicolla in the frige," Tony said, continuing to work on the meat loaf. "The dog's got to eat." As if understanding him, the dog started to bark. "He loves meat loaf. Don't you, King Arthur?"

"His name ought to be Meat Loaf," Donna said, turning from the sink, where she was sloshing dishes around in soapy water.

"Oh, Meat Loaf—that's too much." Florence, who had been pulling apart lettuce, sat down, unable to control her laughter. "Meat Loaf! Why not Bananas, or Grapes and Nuts. Call him Nuts, Tony. Here, Nuts. Peanuts, Cashew Nuts, Walnuts. That's a good name for him, Tony. Walnuts."

Then in unison the three girls started calling the dog different names. "Banana . . . Walnuts . . . Meat Loaf . . . Fruit Salad . . ." Donna wasn't doing the

8

dishes, Flo wasn't making the salad, Evie wasn't setting the table. Nothing was being done. Mrs. Laporte grabbed the meat loaf from Tony's hands, put it back in the refrigerator, and slammed the door.

"Get that dog out of here before I explode," she yelled. "All day those machines pounding in my head, and then to come home to this!"

Fred Laporte was off right after supper to help Bill Taylor lay some drain tile through his cellar in exchange for the help Bill had given him with a washing machine the month before. Tony's mother collapsed into a chair. "I've got to get my wind before I start changing the bed linen," she said to no one in particular. She was sitting in the living room watching a TV comedy and half listening to Tony tell her what a good watchdog Arthur was going to be.

"Mom, you know the way you always worry about robbers and murderers creeping up the railroad tracks in the ravine and getting into the house. Well, no more. Not with King Arthur—"

"Look at that woman," Bev said, pointing to Lucille Ball, who was dancing on the TV screen. "Do you know she's older than me? Lots older! Look at the way she jumps around. How does she do it? I wish I had her energy." She patted the pillow next to her. "Sit down here, Tony honey. I'll comb your hair."

"No." It annoyed Tony that he couldn't get a definite answer from either of his parents. He went out into the hall where King Arthur was tied up. The dog stretched and wagged his tail. Tony knelt down and put his arms around him. "You old hairy, lazy bonebag, don't worry. You big ugly dog. I'm the only one you have to listen to, and I say you stay!"

For a few more days the weather stayed unseasonably warm, and Tony was able to keep the dog in the clubhouse. No problem. Morning and night he brought Arthur his food and water. He had all his friends over to see him and announced that Arthur was going to be their official club mascot.

When Danny Belco called Arthur a large brown turd, a fight broke out between him and Tony. Arthur impressed everyone by nipping at Danny's ankles and tearing his jeans.

"He's a natural protector," Guy Lenny said.

"A one-man dog," Tony said proudly.

Then on Monday the weather turned cold again. Thick, heavy clouds were rising in the west. The wind began to blow and an icy rain fell. Mr. Laporte came home to announce that the temperature was dropping rapidly. There would be snow in the morning. Winter was back—this time to stay.

After supper, Tony went out and brought Arthur up from the clubhouse. He put him in the cellar next to the furnace, where he'd be warm. Tony brought food in a dish, a bowl of water, and a short shaggy rug that his mother would never miss. "Now you've got a cozy place again," he told the dog as he fixed the rug and the food next to the furnace. Tony said nothing to his parents about Arthur being in the cellar. He didn't feel it was necessary.

Sometime after midnight the dog started to whine. Tony slept through the resulting commotion. He heard about it the next morning from both his father and his mother.

The dog's whimpering had waked their landlords. Mrs. Bielic, a stout woman whose cheeks quivered when she walked, was a very light sleeper. She heard the dog at once and woke her husband. They lay there together listening to the creature running back and forth in the cellar. They assumed immediately that the dog belonged to their tenants.

After fifteen or twenty minutes of listening to the dog yipping and racing around the cellar, Mr. Bielic finally got on the phone and called the Laportes.

"Can you imagine how I felt?" Tony's father demanded the next morning as he faced his son. "Bielic wakes me up in the middle of the night and tells me my dog's in the cellar. I didn't know I had a dog in the first place!"

"It ruined our sleep, and on a work night," his mother added.

"You're just lucky you weren't thrown out in the street with that dog," Mr. Laporte said.

"You mean he's gone?" Tony couldn't believe his ears. "You mean you threw him out?"

"That's what I mean," his father said. "And when he tried to come back, I chased him halfway down the block in my bare feet. That dog's just lucky he ran faster than I did, because I would have killed him."

His father might have said more, but he had to drop his wife off at Tex-Lite that morning before he went to work himself, and he didn't have that much time. "Will you hurry up, Bev!" Her 1951 Plymouth, which she usually drove to work, was in the Broadway garage being greased and oiled. "Let's go, slowpoke, or we'll never get across the Boulevard."

Mrs. Laporte pulled on her snow boots and told Tony to eat a good breakfast. "Make sure Evie gets something hot," she called to Flo. Normally she would have started them all toward the breakfast table before she left, but this morning without her car and with her husband yelling, she couldn't take the time.

Tony followed his parents to the stairs, talking defiantly. "I'm finding Arthur and bringing him back," he said. "I'll keep him right in my room."

"That's what *you* say, big mouth, but that's not what *I* say," his father yelled up the stairs. "I'm not having my sleep interrupted by no dog, so forget him. The way I moved him out of here last night he's *never* coming back."

"You're not the boss around here," Tony said furiously. "You can go straight to hell!" But fortunately his father had already gone ahead to warm up the car.

His mother turned at the bottom of the stairs. "There's no use getting upset over a dog, honey. If you find him you'll only have to give him up again." She buttoned up her coat and pulled on her gloves. "Tell your sisters to wear their boots to school." The car horn sounded impatiently. She opened the outside door. "Maybe we can get you something else." Then she was gone.

Tony stood in the cold hallway, letting his bare feet

freeze. "What are you doing out there, Tony?" Flo said. "Come in and shut the door. You're letting in cold air."

Tony didn't reply. He didn't feel the cold. He felt stunned and furious. Arthur was his dog. He'd found him and taken care of him. He loved that dog. He had planned to train the dog to sniff out bombs in airplanes and public buildings. Together they'd go all over on assignment. Maybe it was daydreaming, but it was his dream. When he thought of his dog being driven out of the house in the middle of the night it made him furious. They had no right!

He went inside and dressed quickly. Heavy socks, lined boots, sheepskin winter jacket. He stuck a pair of gloves in his pocket and went out to look for the dog. Flo called after him that he hadn't eaten breakfast. "You know what Mom says. You have to eat something hot in the morning."

Tony didn't reply as he pounded down the back steps. He wasn't going to school till he'd found his dog.

2

CINDY

ON TUESDAY morning when her grandmother brought Cindy Reichert to the bus station it was already snowing. A gently falling curtain of white that set Cindy's mind adrift. When her grandmother insisted on leading her like a child into the bus station, Cindy protested, saying (but only in her head) *I'm perfectly capable of taking care of myself.*

The weekend with her grandmother that she'd looked forward to so much had been a total flop. The communication, the closeness she'd dreamed of—talking, cooking, doing the simplest things together (the things she'd never done with her mother)—none of it had materialized. Grandmother of course had her three dogs, but that wasn't the problem. Even when she and her grandmother had been together, Cindy felt miles away, living alone, locked inside her own head.

The bus station was mobbed. A blast of stale warm air, cigarette fumes, crowds of travelers. Grandmother Reichert gripped Cindy's arm, steering her this way and that until she found an empty bench. "Lucinda, you sit there."

Nobody but her grandmother called her Lucinda. That was her given name, but no one else used it. To her father she was Lucy. To the kids in school, Cindy—even though she wasn't the Cindy type. Cindys had round, pert friendly faces. She had the round face, all right— she was a little too round in all particulars—but she definitely wasn't the friendly type. Picture the corridors of Hendrick Hudson High. The usual mob scene: kids, screams, curses, shouts of jubilation. But wait—one girl walks alone. Cindy Reichert, the school loner, treads softly through the happy hordes, a girl lost in thought, holding her precious books to her bosom, a smile fixed on her face. Alone, forever alone.

Sometimes, even in the midst of people, she thought of herself as a spook from another world, drifting like smoke through open windows—a visitor and a stranger, an observer who saw and recorded everything and touched no one.

"Lucinda, sit down on this bench," Grandmother said. "Are you listening? Sit. I'll see if the bus is going to be on time." Grandmother often talked to Cindy as if she were a child. It was exactly the way she talked to her three dogs. Simple, direct sentences. Simple, direct orders. Not very flattering, but understandable, considering the way Grandmother doted on her dogs. Her whole life was focused on her three dogs—how they were feeling, and whether they were happy and well fed. She had raised three sons (one of them Cindy's father) and now she had three dogs: Mitchel, Ferdie, and Captain.

Cindy fished in her denim carry-all for a stick of gum. (She toted everything in the carry-all: the school books she assured her father she was studying, toothbrush, comb, sunglasses, and lip gloss.) Her father was Grandmother's youngest son. Grandmother's other two sons, Cindy's uncles Hugh and Voss, both lived quite far away with their families. Uncle Hugh was in France, an administrator for the army. Uncle Voss did some kind of medical research at the University of California. Cindy's father was a dermatologist. Although he lived closer to Grandmother than any of her other sons and their families, he didn't see Grandmother much more than Uncle Voss or Uncle Hugh. Cindy's father hated traveling, visiting, or having his routine disrupted in any way. There were three things in the world he had a passion for: his work, playing golf, and playing the cello.

Cindy and her father got along perfectly, but she definitely wasn't one of his passions. She was convinced she was exactly like him. Cool, and complete unto herself. He didn't care much for people and neither did she. He preferred his own company, and so did she. Cindy played the piano and wrote poetry and went to the movies. If she liked a movie she could see it four or five times—or even ten times—without tiring of it. (She thought she might want to be an actress someday, but she wasn't completely sure about that.)

She had been raised by her father because her mother had died when Cindy was three. She'd seen pictures of her mother, of course, and heard the family stories. Her mother had been a beautiful and talented woman; her death was a tragedy. Cindy thought of her mother every day. When she was feeling weird enough, she talked to her. Cindy was sure her mother's influence would have made her a more outgoing generous person, kinder to other people in all ways.

Sometimes when she was in a really self-critical mood, she would look at herself, and it was as if she were looking into the polished sphere of a doorknob—her face came out with a knob of a nose and a wide mouth, and her eyes where her ears belonged. Ugh! She knew she spent too much time thinking about herself, because the more she thought, the more wrong things she saw.

"Lucinda," Grandmother said, coming back from studying the big board of arrivals and departures, "the bus to Malone is going to be two hours late. This foul weather! Do you want to wait? Do you want to come home with me? Maybe that would be best, dear." She pulled up the zipper of Cindy's coat and fussed with her collar. "I wish you'd dress better." Her eyes went critically over Cindy's worn dungarees, the loose black turtleneck sweater, her sensible but unfashionable rubber boots, and her shapeless brown coat. All part of

Cindy's anonymous costume. In no way was she interested in drawing attention to herself.

"I'll wait here, Grandmother," she said reassuringly.
"You go home. I know you don't like to leave the dogs
for too long. I'll be all right." She squeezed her grandmother's shoulder. "Go, Grandmother, go!" She was
talking dog-talk, too.

Her grandmother gave her the tin of cookies she'd
baked. "Chocolate chip. I baked them last night. Don't
shake them, or they'll be all crumbs. Don't forget to call
as soon as you get home. Don't talk to strangers. Give
my love to your father, and come again soon." She
patted the top of Cindy's head, and then she was gone.

Cindy was relieved when her grandmother left.
Being with her all weekend, trying to please her, being
careful what she said, even of what she thought, Cindy
felt that she'd been pushed into a corner of her mind.
Now she could feel herself expanding like a raisin turning into a grape. Or was she thinking of a prune? Alone,
she could occupy herself freely, pleasing only herself,
arranging things the way she liked, working out her
little strategies.

She bought a magazine, two chocolate almond bars,
and a package of gumdrops. The room was slowly filling
up with more and more people, bulky in their coats,
jackets, and boots. It was hot, steamy, and noisy.
Through the corridor leading to the outside door, Cindy
saw the snow falling silently. She sat down on a bench
and flipped through the magazine, nibbling on an almond bar. A woman with two little babies sat down next

to her. Then a tall blondish kid planted himself in front of her. He wore a denim work outfit and a blue knit cap pulled down over his long hair. He stared at Cindy, rocking back and forth on his heels, seeming very pleased with himself.

When things like that happened in school and Cindy felt she was being ridiculed or mocked, she got away as quickly as she could. But the way this kid was staring at her she could only stare back. It was a stare-down, and he was winning. She had the urge to get up and shake him by the ears. Who did he think he was looking at so hard? But as with a lot of really powerful urges she'd had in her life, she didn't do anything.

Instead she turned so she wouldn't have to look at him. And then, after a minute or so, she got up as if she had someplace important to go and headed for the ladies' room. When she came out she saw that her bus was now posted on the board as being nearly three hours late. Snow storms off the Great Lakes. It didn't seem that bad outside, though. She bought a couple more chocolate bars and a bag of Fritos. When she glanced around, the tall blond kid was giving her the Stare again. She picked up her bag and went outside.

It was colder than she'd expected, too cold to just stand around and wait three more hours for the bus. She was tired of waiting in that stale, stuffy bus station, tired of that smart-alec boy. On impulse—that's all it was— she walked across the street and stuck out her thumb. She'd hitchhiked before. The bus service in the suburb where she and her father lived was really rotten. Her father didn't know she hitched, and she was pretty sure he wouldn't care for the idea at all. To her, it was as simple, or as complicated, as crossing the street. If you were careful, you made it safely to the other side; but if you were careless, anything could happen. Who could say that riding a bus was so safe? Buses had accidents, too.

She had to admit, however, there was something a little masochistic about her hitchhiking. Not the dangers —they were real enough, though probably exaggerated by anxious parents. No. What was pure torture for her was getting into a car and knowing she had to communicate with another person. The first few times she had hitched, she sat there like a lump on a log. The driver didn't say anything and she didn't say anything. Her tongue felt stiff as wood and there was an obstruction in her throat and she could barely sit still for wanting OUT. It was *that* awful. The only word she finally managed was a grunt of thanks as she threw herself out of the car.

To avoid this torture she worked out a few key phrases that generally got things going. "Hello! I'm Cindy Reichert! What's your name?" Once the driver started talking she could sit back and listen, or even answer questions, which she never minded as much.

Three cars passed her, and she'd begun to wonder if she ought to go back into the bus station when a black VW rolled up. There was a man at the wheel. "How far you going?" she said, opening the door. There were college stickers on the windows.

"Sandy Creek," he said. "Climb in."

She settled herself in the seat, the denim bag and the tin of cookies in her lap. "Hi! My name is Cindy Reichert. What's yours?"

"David," he said. He looked safe enough—about twenty, she thought—wiry, and wearing black-rimmed glasses. The first thing he did was to start lecturing her on the dangers of thumbing.

"How old are you, Cindy? Do your parents know you're hitching? Aren't you worried? What if you were in a car with a guy who tried to do something? What if I was a pervert? I'm not, but you never can tell. They say they're all over. You're lucky a nice guy like me came along."

Cindy felt embarrassed the way she often did when people paid too much personal attention to her. "The weather . . ." she said by way of explanation, gesturing vaguely to the snow coming down steadily outside. "The bus was late, and I was trying to make up time."

He wiped moisture off the windshield with his hand. "You don't fool around in this country." Big brother David. He was back to lecturing her. "This is Snow Belt country you're in now. It snows here when it doesn't snow anyplace else, tons and tons of snow. It's the Great Lakes. Cold Canadian air sweeps over the warmer lake and sucks up water that turns to heavy clouds that dump snow all over these leeward hills."

Cindy looked toward the hills. They weren't very high. Gray and indistinct.

"My girl lives up there," he said. "Toward Tug

Hill. You ever hear of the Tug Hill area? That's really no-man's-land. When I go see her, eight months of the year I go by snowmobile."

"That sounds like fun," Cindy said.

"You have a boyfriend?" She shook her head. "Still young and innocent," he said.

Cindy said nothing. They drove in silence for a long while. At least the lectures had stopped. At a crossroads he pulled up on the shoulder. "This is where I turn off." The snow was coming down steadily. The lights of oncoming cars shone dimly through the snow.

"Which way is north?" Cindy said.

"Just stay on the highway. This is Route Eleven. It goes all the way up to the Canadian border. Gee, I hate to put you out in this weather. Why don't you come home with me?"

Uh-uh, Cindy thought, it's happening. First the talk about perverts, then boyfriends, and now this. She gripped her sack and the cookie tin in one hand and opened the car door with the other. "Thanks a lot. Appreciate this—"

"No, wait a minute, Cindy." He reached across to hold the door shut. "I mean it. You don't know this territory. When it snows, it snows. You don't have to worry, my mother's at home. She'll be glad to take you. . . ."

He probably meant every word he said, but there wasn't a chance in the world that she'd go with him. "Thanks," she said. "Really, I'll be all right." She got out, and a moment later she was standing on the road watching his red taillights disappear in the snow.

For a long time there was nothing, not a light or a car in any direction. Snow fell heavily into a thick silence. Cindy had never felt so alone and cut off in her life. Gradually she became aware of the cars cautiously coming toward her, emerging from the dusk, silent as gray shadows in a dream. She pulled up her collar, hunched her shoulders, and when the next car appeared, stuck out her thumb.

3

THE HITCHHIKER

WHEN TONY walked out on the bridge the cold caught him by surprise. The wind was sharper here, whistling under the abutments. "Here, boy," he yelled. "Good boy, Arthur. Here, Arthur." The wind whipped the words from his mouth. He went further, past the bridge to the stores at the end of Bridge Street. A fine, thin snow was falling, etching every crack and crevice. Danny Belco, on his way to school, hailed Tony. He waved Danny on. He wasn't going to school until he found his dog.

He crossed between the mattress shop and shoe store, over to Broadway, and back down past the Broadway Garage, where he could see his mother's blue 1951 Plymouth on the lot. He crossed the street and asked

Frank Beach, the mechanic on duty, if he'd seen his dog. Frank was working the pumps outside, gassing up a green Dodge Lancer. "Nope." Frank shook his head. "Too cold to think about dogs."

Tony crisscrossed the neighborhood—Summit, Townsend, Bridge—stopping to ask anyone he met if they'd seen a medium-sized brown dog. Twice he checked the ravine, climbing down to the clubhouse, where the wind was really howling. He went home to warm up and use the bathroom; his Aunt Irene's black Olds was in the driveway. She saw him before he could get away.

"What are you doing home? You're supposed to be in school." She peered at him suspiciously. Like her sister, his mother, she had four of her own, except hers were all boys, and she knew every trick in the book. "You're playing hookey, aren't you? Don't give me that innocent look, Anthony. You're not sweet-talking your mother now. This is me, Aunt Irene. You get to school, on-the-double. I'm going to call the principal's office in fifteen minutes, and you better be there. So move, big boy!" She got into her car, rolling down the window to say, "You go to school, Anthony, you hear me?"

"Yes," he said, following her as she backed out to the street, but the moment she was gone he went the opposite way. For the next hour he went over all the streets he'd covered already, without finding a trace of the dog. He was really cold now, stamping his feet and blowing on his fingers. Stubbornly he refused to give up the search. The longer it went on, the angrier he became. They hadn't even waked Tony to ask him if he knew some place for the dog. No, they'd simply kicked the dumb mutt out into the night because he made a little noise and woke up the landlords. As if Tony cared about the Bielics, always worrying about their house. When Mr. Bielic came upstairs to collect the rent on the first of the month, he would look at the floors and the walls. A little crack in the plaster and he had a fit. "Oh, ho, what's this, Mrs. Laporte!" He'd stretch his lips and shake his finger playfully, but he meant it. His precious house meant more to him than anything. More than a dog, for sure. And Tony's father had fallen right in with him. Tony's blood boiled every time he thought about it. His dog out in the snow, just because he'd made a little noise! What right did they have? It was *his* dog, nobody else's. Hot rage swept over him. Rage at his parents. It was the dog, but it was more than the dog. He didn't want to go home. He'd never go home. Once he let himself go, thinking this way, there was no bottom to the feeling of betrayal.

He went back to the gas station. Frank was in the garage. "Is it cold!" Frank said. "Find your dog yet?" Tony shook his head.

"Too bad." Frank blew his nose in a red handkerchief. "Anyone who works on a day like this has gotta be crazy. Right, kid?"

"Is my mother's car ready yet?" Tony asked. "I thought I'd warm it up if it was ready. Have you got the key?" He watched Frank take his mother's set of keys from the grease-stained key board behind the cash register.

"Put them back when you're done," Frank said.

Tony pocketed the keys and walked out to his mother's car. He was too young for a junior license, but ever since he'd been old enough to reach the pedals, he'd been driving cars around empty shopping centers and in the country around his Uncle Leonard's place.

He slid in behind the wheel. The seat was like ice. He liked his mother's car, especially the rounded, old-fashioned bumblebee look that cars had back in the late forties and early fifties. He preferred it to the new look-alike cars. The car started hard, sputtering and coughing, but once the engine caught, it idled down quietly, and quickly warmed up. Tony backed it to one of the gas pumps and filled the gas tank. He went inside and told Frank to charge it. Then, while Frank was busy with another customer, Tony got back into the car and drove out of the lot. He was past his house, turning right at Townsend before his heart quieted down.

During the time he had been looking for Arthur, another plan had been forming in his mind. He had the car. For what they'd done, he'd give them something to worry about. He'd show them that they couldn't push him around and get away with it.

He turned off Townsend and down Sand Street into a more residential section. He was a little nervous at first. He'd never driven in the city before. Not that he had any doubts about his driving ability. He knew he was good.

Without hesitation, he swung on to Interstate 81 leading north to Canada. His Uncle Leonard lived near Watertown. That was where he'd go. Uncle Leonard was his father's youngest brother, a bachelor everyone in the family called Perry Como because he looked like the singer and liked to play golf. His uncle was always doing interesting things. He lived in a trailer and had a boat. Tony had been fishing and hunting with him many times, and he always had rod or gun ready for Tony when he came. His uncle would be glad to see him. Didn't he always tease the family, telling them he'd take the boy to live with him any time they got tired of him? Well, now Tony was tired of them. After what they'd done to his dog, he didn't want to live at home again.

Tony began to feel really good for the first time. He felt bad whenever he remembered Arthur, but he was thinking of other things, too. Tony expected his uncle would bawl him out for driving without a license, but once he was there Uncle Leonard would have to be impressed with the perfect trip he'd made.

Driving the car did something for Tony. He loved driving and became completely involved in the road and the feel of the car in his hands. The heater was throwing good heat, the radio was on, and he kept to a smooth, steady fifty-five miles an hour, keeping all the way to the right in case the troopers were out. He felt free and wide-awake, forgetting everything but the car and humming along with the radio. Even the snow that had begun to slide across the windshield like sand didn't dampen his mood. It was a cold, dry snow, the kind that blew off the road as fast as it fell.

Every once in a while Tony glanced sharply in the rearview mirror. When he was sure that nobody was behind him or coming toward him, he swerved suddenly from one lane to the other and then back to his own lane

28

again. The car behaved perfectly. Tony slapped the wheel and whooped. He could do anything he wanted with this car. If only his friends could see and admire him. It brought to mind a daydream of his—rescuing someone from great danger. He'd thought of it more than once. Jumping into a car that was rolling out of control, a school bus, maybe . . . There'd be all these terrified kids in it. He'd know just what to do. Grab the wheel, turn off the ignition, pull out the emergency brake! He'd read about a boy on a school bus doing exactly that when the driver had a heart attack. This kid had brought the bus to a safe stop and saved about thirty lives. He was a real hero. Tony would do the same thing if he ever had the chance. He'd act decisively; he wouldn't be the least bit afraid.

Maybe someday he'd have a chance to do the same thing on a plane. What if there was a crazy hijacker who was holding the hostess and the pilots as prisoners. They had tried to disarm him, and he'd shot both pilots. Killed one, but the other, bleeding badly, was still conscious. Tony had seen that once on television. He imagined himself on that plane, this time with the hijacker dead (the pilot had shot him before he, himself, died) and everybody hysterical. Tony would come forward and coolly take the controls. The wounded pilot would tell him what to do, and he'd bring the plane down smooth as cream.

Newspaper reporters would mob him, the TV cameramen shooting over the heads of the crowd. Probably the President would call him at home that night. "Tony? This is the President of the United States. I just want to tell you what we as a nation owe you for your bravery in the face of terrible danger. I want to say thank you for all the people of the United States. It's citizens like you who—"

Tony glanced at the instrument panel. He was going eighty miles an hour. He let up on the gas and again drove more carefully, keeping to his own lane. The traffic was light as he moved steadily northward. Between breaks in the music and advertising, the announcer kept giving snow warnings, telling people not to travel unless absolutely necessary.

For some time the snow had been driving against the windshield, hammering the windows in an endless, hypnotic barrage. Tony was afraid that he'd forget the road or go too fast again. When a state trooper passed him, giving him a long look, he made a quick decision and turned off at the next exit to use the old state highway 11, which roughly paralleled the Interstate. He'd often heard his father comment that the troopers didn't bother with Route 11 traffic now that they had the Interstate to patrol.

He turned on the headlights and peered ahead, thinking of his uncle's surprise when he saw him. He passed the hitchhiker before he registered what he was seeing—a muffled figure on the road's shoulder. It was a rotten time for any guy to be on the road. Tony stopped, shoved the shift into reverse, and backed up, blasting the horn.

The hitchhiker pulled open the door and slid into the front seat, bringing in bundles and blowing snow. Tony nodded to him as he shifted into first and started forward again. The hitchhiker pulled down the collar of his jacket and brushed snow off his arms and shoulders. He took his mittens off and kneaded his fingers in front of the warm air blasting in from the heater. Then for the first time he spoke. "Hi. I'm Cindy Reichert. What's your name?"

4

CINDY TAKES THE WHEEL

THE MINUTE Cindy was in the car and warming up she started talking. A regular talking jag. She was *that* glad to be inside after being out in that snow. With the falling snow piling up on her shoulders and hair, creeping up over her boots, she'd begun to imagine herself buried under a mountain of snow. She'd still be standing there next spring, to be discovered when her frozen head slowly emerged from the thawing snow. Yes, she was glad to be inside! That little heater in the car threw the warmest warmth she'd ever felt. This was probably the nicest car she'd ever been in. She sat back and patted the cushions. "This car is old, but really beautiful," she said to the boy driving. "You must be happy driving this car."

"You're going to Malone?" he said. He'd already asked her once. She nodded. "Well, I'll take you as far as Watertown, even though it's out of my way."

"I appreciate that."

He glanced at her. "You're lucky I picked you up. A lot of people don't pick up hitchhikers. Especially girls."

"I know and I appreciate." Cindy was being rapidly cooled off by his manner.

"I can't see girls hitching. How come you're hitching anyway? Your parents mustn't care much for you. My father would whip my sisters good if he ever caught them doing that."

"My father doesn't whip me, and he doesn't know I'm hitching. This is my own idea," she replied coolly. The thought of her father whipping her was ludicrous. What sort of family did this boy come from?

"You must be really stupid," he said.

"Oh, thank you very much!" Her luck hadn't changed at all. He was like that boy in the bus station— one of those good-looking, egotistical boys who thought they could say anything to a girl and get away with it. Probably spoiled rotten by his good looks. The excitement, the gladness she'd felt on finally getting a ride—all of it was gone now.

The car tunneled through the snow, the headlights illuminating snow and more snow piling up on the road, on fences, bushes, and fields. She really had the worst luck when it came to hitching. First the teacher pervert, and now this conceited know-it-all. It was enough to make her swear off hitching forever.

33

She reached into her denim bag and got out one of the chocolate bars she'd bought at the bus station. She pulled off the paper. "That smells good," he said. "I haven't eaten all day."

She shared the chocolate bars and the bag of Fritos with him. He finished the Fritos, tipping the bag up to catch the last crumbs before handing her the empty cellophane wrapper. "Thanks," he said. The feeling in the car was a little more companionable after that. He didn't seem as obnoxious. He told her his name was Tony.

"You really haven't eaten anything else, Tony?" she said. "Why don't we stop?" She pointed to a diner at the edge of the road, its neon sign casting a pink glow in the snow-filled air. "Let me buy, to pay for the ride."

"Anything I want?"

"Sure, why not."

"You don't have enough money to pay for what I could eat."

"I'll take a chance," she said.

The parking lot was half full of cars and trucks. Tony ran ahead to the diner. When Cindy caught up to him he was standing outside the door, peering in through the steamy windows. Cindy looked in over his shoulder. The diner was crowded. A plump waitress in a white uniform with a lacy handkerchief pinned above her breast pocket was talking to a couple of troopers in gray pants and gray jackets. They were hunched over the counter, and their wide black belts and the guns in their leather holsters were plainly visible.

"Come on, let's go in," Cindy said. "It's cold out here." She opened the door, feeling the diner's heat on her face. One of the troopers turned and looked at them.

"It's too jammed in there," Tony said abruptly. He pushed her aside and ran back to the car. He was going without her! She ran after him, getting snow down her boots. She was barely in the car before he had it on the road again, going so fast he was skidding and sliding across the road.

"What's the matter with you?" she said. "Why'd you run like that? Is that some kind of trick? I thought you were hungry!"

"I changed my mind, okay? Bug off. You didn't have to come if you didn't want to."

"You didn't give me much choice! My stuff was in the car."

"You want out?" he said.

"Out where?" The diner had disappeared behind them. Around them there was nothing but the bleakness of the road. Cindy didn't know what to think about this boy now. Friendly one minute, hostile the next. Had he been scared of the troopers? She glanced over at him. Was he too young to be driving? How old did you have to be to drive in New York State? Looking at him again, she didn't think he was old enough to have a license in any state.

"You're too young to have a driving license, aren't you?" she said. "Do you even have a learner's permit?"

"What are you afraid of? I can drive."

So she was right. "You shouldn't be driving without

35

a license." Something else occurred to her. "Did you steal this car?"

"Steal it!" His voice shot up. "It's my mother's. Listen . . ." He began talking excitedly about a dog he'd found that his family wouldn't let him keep, and how he took the car and wasn't going home again. All this at the top of his lungs.

"All right," she said, "don't get excited, watch the road. I don't want to end up in a ditch." She rubbed the fog off the inside of the windshield with her hand. She was sure now that he was too young, even younger than she was. It had been a mistake getting into this car, but then hitching today had turned out to be one mistake after another. She promised herself that as soon as they got to someplace civilized she was getting out and not hitching again, even if she had to call her father to come and get her.

The driving was getting really bad. Gusts of snow flew into the windshield, making it impossible at times to see anything. Tony sat forward on the edge of his seat, peering ahead, both hands gripping the wheel. Cindy was doing the same, wiping his windshield when it fogged over, being careful not to say anything to distract him or start him yelling again.

A snowplow, huge and ghostly, lurched toward them, red lights flashing, spattering the car with a barrage of sand and salt as it passed. Ahead, a long line of cars were piled up behind another snowplow which was slowly clearing the road. They were crawling along, and it made Tony impatient. He hit the wheel.

"We'll never get anywhere this way!" Suddenly he turned sharply off the highway and down a side road.

"What are you doing?" Cindy asked. "Where are you going?"

"Taking a short cut. You want to get to Watertown, don't you?"

"A short cut. What do you mean by that? You didn't tell me anything about a short cut. What was wrong with the road we were on?"

He didn't reply. He was leaning forward concentrating on his driving. "In a few miles, watch out for a little white building with a green tin roof. That used to be a country school. Once we see that, we turn right; and then we only have to go over a hill and down over two bridges and turn left, and then turn right again. That's Little Black Creek Road, and we'll be heading straight into Watertown."

"You made it all up," Cindy said. It sounded so unreal to her, like something out of a fairy tale. "I don't like this," she said uneasily.

"You want to get to the bus station, don't you? That's what you want, isn't it? So just let me do the driving."

The bus station. What she wouldn't have given to be there! She thought of its crowded, steamy warmth, the candy machines and phones. But what was the use of thinking of it? She sat back, telling herself it would only be a little longer. "As long as you know where you are," she said.

"I know this country like the back of my hand," he

37

boasted. He told her that he, his father, and his Uncle Leonard had hunted rabbit, pheasant, and deer all through these hills. He was going to his uncle's as soon as he dropped her at the bus station. "I'm going to live with my uncle from now on," he said.

"Okay," Cindy said. "Fine. I understand." She didn't want him to talk. She wanted him to concentrate on his driving. The wind was buffeting the car, and there were times when they couldn't see the road. Ever since he'd turned off the main highway, Cindy had begun to feel that theirs was the only car on the road. They seemed to be the only people crazy enough to drive in such weather. Once she grabbed his arm because she thought he was going off the road. "You're on the wrong side!"

He jerked his arm away. "I saw it. You don't have to worry. I'm doing it on purpose. Riding the center." A little later he said they'd passed the schoolhouse and had turned right, going over the hill. "Keep a lookout for the first bridge," he ordered.

She didn't see any of the things he was talking about. Her eyes were fixed straight ahead, but her heart was in her mouth. The wind was driving snow in great sheets, piling drifts across the road so high that at times Tony had to weave to one side and then the other to keep going ahead. On Cindy's side of the car the land dropped away like the side of a cliff. She sat tensely on the edge of her seat, unable to speak. The car was fish-tailing down the hill.

"There's a bridge at the foot," he said. "The one I told you about."

She wiped the fog from his side of the windshield and then her side. She couldn't see anything. No bridge, no road,—nothing. "Where are we?" she said. "Do you know where we are? I don't think we're even on a road."

"There's a bridge here somewhere," he said. "Maybe I made a wrong turn. We'll go ahead slow till we see where we are."

Fifteen minutes passed, and they still hadn't come off whatever side road they were on. Cindy kept wiping the windshield and the window on her side, looking and trying to see something through the impenetrable curtain of snow. She thought of telling Tony to stop, but there was no place to stop. In front of them, in back of them, on all sides, she could see only snow—falling, blowing snow, piling up into incredible drifts. They hadn't passed another car in at least half an hour. There were no houses, barns, stores, diners, or animals in sight. And Cindy became aware of something else—there were no wires, not a telephone or a light pole. Nothing. It was as if they'd driven off the edge of the world.

"Which way?" Tony said. They'd come to a level place where the road seemed to divide. "Right or left?"

"Go . . . left," she said, and crossed her fingers.

"I'm going right." The car bumped and jumped and slid. They were rolling down a hill. Cindy put her hand to her mouth. They were off the road, she was sure of that now, and out of control. She sat on the edge of the seat, gripping it with both hands, as the car lurched and tossed down the hill and across the fields. There were wooded hills rising on both sides of them and more woods in front of them.

"You idiot," she cried in desperation. "You bragging idiot. You've got us lost!" And without thinking, in a fury of fear and anger, she grabbed the wheel and twisted it out of his hand.

5

THIS AWFUL SNOW

Tony knocked the girl's hand away and grabbed the wheel. The car was bumping across the field, out of control. He hung onto the wheel, twisting one way and then the other. He didn't see the rocks and debris half buried in the snow until they hit, scraping, ramming into the boulders that threw the car half up in the air before they came to a stop. They were both thrown violently forward. "Holy Mary," Tony said. "Holy Mother Mary. Oh, God."

The silence in the aftermath of the motor's dying was eerie. Only the heater whirred. Tony automatically switched it off, then sat there dazed, unable to think. The wind had been knocked out of him. He didn't look at the girl. His father was going to kill him when he found out he'd ruined the car. He would absolutely rip off his head.

The girl was crumpled against the door, her hands over her face. "Why'd you do that?" he said. It was her fault, all her fault. Rage spurted through him. "You dumb cluck! You stupid female! You crazy bitch!" He kept at her even when she didn't respond. She shouldn't have grabbed the wheel. He knew he'd made a wrong turn, but he would have found the right way. He wasn't a complete dope. He'd seen that the power poles along the side of the road had disappeared. He hadn't said anything because he'd been hoping to come back on the road again where he'd recognize landmarks. But this snow! This awful snow. It had changed everything, splattering over the road and the trees and the fences, blowing against the windshield, obscuring his vision and his sense of direction, obliterating the landmarks he would have recognized, until he'd lost all sense of where they were. She'd fixed everything by getting hysterical and snatching the wheel, getting them marooned in this field.

They'd never get out alone now, not in a thousand years. They'd have to wait to be towed out. And when his father found out where they were and what he'd done to the car . . . He wasn't thinking about his Uncle Leonard anymore. What was he going to tell his father? And his mother! It was her car. She loved her car.

"You see what you did," he said furiously. The girl still hadn't spoken. "You!" He poked her in the side.

42

"I'm talking to *you*." He thought maybe she was crying, but when she turned toward him her face was covered with blood. "Holy Mary. What happened to you?"

She looked at the blood on her hand and then felt it on her face. She pulled the mirror around to look at herself, touching her face with a handkerchief. She'd split her left eyebrow. She held the handkerchief to her forehead.

"That's not so bad," he said. "It looked worse than it was. You'll be all right."

She turned toward him, her face white and cold. She pointed through the snowflecked windshield to the nearly dark wooded hills rising on all sides of them. "Do you have any idea at all where we are now?"

"We'll be all right," he said.

"We're in a terrible mess," she said. "We're lost and nobody knows where we are."

He wanted to get away from her and the infuriating things she was saying. He wanted to get out of the car and walk around, look at things for himself. But the door on his side was jammed shut against the rocks, and he didn't want to slide by her and go out her side. "We're not lost," he said stubbornly, but he wasn't so sure. He had to think. It was hard. His head hurt. It was dark already, and there was so much snow. The snow fell and fell. It fell silently without stopping, leaving him frustrated and angry. Why didn't it stop! He turned the key in the ignition. The motor whined.

She was watching him. "It won't start," she said. "We're lost, and you can't start the car. We'll freeze to death."

43

He wanted to contradict her loudly, set her straight, show her a thing or two. "I know where I am." He pointed to the hill in front of them. "That's Bear Hill," he said, plucking a name randomly from his mind. "And on your side, that's Slant Rock. And over here where we are now, there's a brook running. Deer Brook, that's the name. Deer Brook."

She gave him a level, dubious look, but then craned her head to look out her side. "I can't see any slanting rock," she said.

"Of course not, stupid! The snow's covering it. But it's there."

She gave him another of those long, disquieting looks. "Let's get something straight. I told you my name. Lucinda. You can call me Cindy. My name is not 'stupid.' "

"Can't you take a joke?" he said.

"You don't know me that well, and you're not that funny. In fact, you're very unfunny. I'm sorry I ever got into this car with you. It was probably the worst mistake of my life. I only hope I get out of this alive."

It was all he could do not to smack her. He'd never felt like hitting anyone as much as he wanted to hit this girl. "Don't be a dope," he said through taut lips. "Somebody's going to come along pretty soon. I'm not worried. As soon as they plow out the main road, they'll start on these smaller roads, and—"

"You don't know what you're talking about," she interrupted. "You took a car that wasn't yours. You drove it without a license. You got us lost in the middle of nowhere. Everything you do is wrong."

She wouldn't shut up. She kept at him until he began shouting, his voice louder than hers. "Shut your mouth! I'll kick you out of this car. It's my car. I can kick you out if I want to!"

"You aren't going to do anything to me," she said. "If we were anywhere except in this God-forsaken place, I'd be out of this car in a second. Believe me, I'd be so happy to be anywhere else in the world, except with you!"

Furious, frustrated, he punched her denim carry-all. "Open the door and get out of here," he yelled. He shoved her against the door. "Go on! Out! Out, out!"

Her eyes opened wide in surprise and shock. He could see he'd frightened her, and he was glad; but she didn't burst into tears and yell bloody murder for her mother as his sisters would have done. Instead she reached into her carry-all and brought out a thick school book. She faced him, holding the book in both hands. She was going to fight.

"Nobody's ever hit me before in my life, and you're not going to start. I'll get out when I'm good and ready, and not before." She held the book high, daring him to make another move.

He reached across her, trying to open the door on her side. She cracked him smartly across the hand with the book. He jerked back and punched her in the arm. Instead of breaking down in sobs, she threw the book into his face, catching him painfully across the nose. Furiously he opened the window and threw her book into the snow. A blast of cold wind and snow cut across his cheek, and he rolled up the window fast.

45

"You're a bully," she said. "I never in my life met anyone as mean and rotten as you."

He turned so he was facing away from her. His nose hurt, but he wasn't going to give her the satisfaction of putting his hand to it. He made up his mind he wouldn't fight with her again. He wouldn't talk to her, either. Not that he was afraid of her. Hell, no. He could handle her with one hand behind his back.

For a long time they sat apart from each other. His legs began to feel cramped and he wanted to stretch, but he wasn't going to be the first one to make a move. It was also getting colder and colder in the car and his toes felt numb. Let her freeze. He wasn't going to start the motor. They'd see how tough she really was!

"Did you turn into a snowman?" Her voice startled him. She'd pulled her collar up and wound her scarf around her face. "I'm cold." She rearranged herself so she was sitting on her feet, her hands tucked under her coat. "Try to start the car and give us some heat. I'm freezing."

"Don't tell me what to do," he said. But the cold seeping under the door and through the floor was affecting him, too. He turned the ignition key. A red light blinked on the instrument panel.

"Won't it start?" she asked. She watched as he turned the key on and off, on and off, pumping gas, leaving his foot down on the pedal, then lifting it off. He wasn't sure which way was right. He only knew that after he'd tried the ignition a half dozen times he was sweating, half cursing, half praying. He could smell gasoline. He was flooding the engine. They would have to wait.

"If you can't start the car, we're going to freeze," Cindy said in a remote voice. "We might be here a week before they find us, and when they do we'll be frozen to death."

He hated her. She was crazy. They were going to be out of here at the latest tomorrow. "Somebody's going to come," he insisted. "We're going to be found."

"No. Not a single car has come by while we've been here. We're not on a road. If we were on a road, we'd have a chance. But we're nowhere! We don't know how far away the road is. It might be a mile away or five miles, or even more."

"Maybe there's a car coming right now," Tony said loudly. He put up a hand. "Shut up and listen!" He'd have liked to hold her mouth shut the way he did to Donna when she babbled too much. He raised his head and listened tensely. What he wouldn't have given to see or hear a car or a snowplow. Anything to prove her wrong. He listened, concentrating and straining; but except for the steely, wind-driven patter of snow against metal and glass, there was nothing.

"You see. There's nobody," she said.

"Shut up. It's too soon," he said. "They'll come. It's still snowing and everyone's off the road and staying home right now. The snowplows will be out later."

"You hope," she said. She blew on her hands. "Try the key again, maybe it'll start now."

He turned the key. The engine flared to life. "It

was flooded before," he said, feeding gas and listening to the muffled sound of the exhaust.

For the first time she smiled at him. "That sounds so good." She put her hands out to the heater. "I'm so glad you got it started."

He climbed over the seat and forced open the back door on his side. "Where are you going?" she said. He didn't answer. He was down on his knees clearing the snow away from the exhaust pipe. Then, opening the back door again, he removed a piece of cardboard his father kept there and put it on the outside of the radiator to make the water heat up faster. Shaking as much snow off himself as he could, he got back in the car and crawled into the front seat. He'd only glanced at the damage outside; the whole side of the car was punched in. There was no use thinking about it now.

"Where'd you learn that?" Cindy said. "That was smart." It was the first time she'd spoken to him with respect.

He shrugged. "I know a lot more than that."

The car heated rapidly. The cold air still came in through the cracks, but it was bearable. Tony glanced at the gas gauge. The indicator hovered around the half mark. Cindy was holding her feet up to the heater. He considered turning the engine on and off to conserve fuel, but then he thought that when the storm cleared— by morning, for sure—they'd find help, so why bother?

"Don't you think we ought to open a window, Tony?" Cindy said. "There might be carbon monoxide leaking in."

"So open it." He leaned back against the seat and

closed his eyes. He told himself that when he woke up it would be morning, the snowstorm would have ended, and they'd be rescued. He listened to the uneven throbbing of the engine—like the furnace at home, he thought. In an hour or two his parents and his sisters would realize he was gone. Did his father come straight home from work Tuesday night, or was that the night he ate lasagna on Third Street before he went to his union executive board meeting? Even so, his father would be home by ten thirty or eleven at the latest, and when his mother told him that Tony had taken the car, his father would throw a fit. They'd probably check his friends' homes before they'd think something had really happened to him and call the police.

Would they ever guess that he'd started for his Uncle Leonard's? He couldn't tell about his parents. Sometimes they acted as if they didn't think of anything, and other times they put things together fast. What about the night he'd slept in the clubhouse earlier that fall, in October? He'd had a fight with his father and he'd walked out of the house, telling himself they could darn well figure out where he was. But when he came in the following morning for breakfast, expecting all hell to break loose, his mother was calm and his father gave him a cheery hello. They'd known where he was right along and hadn't minded at all. So maybe they weren't worrying about him now, either.

Tony sighed and looked out the window at the relentlessly falling snow, the dark luminescent sky that pressed down on them like a suffocating blanket. What a mess! As he started to doze off, panic raced away with him. What if it snowed for two or three days? Or even a week, as Cindy had said. He wouldn't admit it to her, but those things weren't unknown in this snow country. He pushed away the terrifying thoughts. He wouldn't think that way. "It's going to be okay," he told himself. "It's going to be okay. It's going to be okay."

6

A NIGHT OF ICE

IN THE DREAM it was night and the streets were empty and cold. Cindy passed a bus, its windows filled with a cold greenish light. Three men were sitting inside, looking straight ahead, their faces green as ducks. A woman urged Cindy to get in, but she was afraid. She ran across the street and up on a wide porch of a house. Through a window she saw a boy about her age motioning to her. She tried the door. It opened. She was enveloped in a delicious heat. As she stood in the darkened hallway a door above her opened. A man all in white appeared at the head of the stairs, sitting up in a hospital bed. "Stop! Don't move," he ordered. "I'll call the police."

Cindy awoke suddenly, an anxious, tight feeling in her throat. For a moment she didn't know where she was. Her arms and legs were stiff and cramped, her neck felt broken. Slowly she became aware of the car, the cramped position in which she'd been sleeping. Through the frosted windshield a silvery gray light sifted into the car.

It was morning, but it could have been twilight. Cindy felt as if a lifetime had passed—heavy frozen hours—a night of ice. It was still snowing. In the back seat she saw Tony's dark inert shape. *Carbon monoxide.* The thought flashed in her head like a white light. He lay there so heavily, lifelessly, like a sack. She couldn't hear his breathing. The back of her own head felt strange, as if wires were being pulled. Her eyelids drooped. She could feel every bone in her body, fragile and brittle as straws.

"Tony!" Cindy rolled down the window and gulped icy air. "Tony, wake up. Are you all right?"

He struggled up, blinked, and rubbed the saliva off his mouth. "What's the matter? Why'd you wake me?" He sounded cross and not the least bit dead. "Shut the window, for God's sake!"

"I'm afraid of carbon monoxide poisoning. I thought you were being affected."

"Oh, shit." He lay back again.

She sat there with the window open, drawing in icy gulps of the snow-thickened dawn air. The wind had died down. The snow fell like a veil of silvery ice into a silence unlike any she'd ever known before. There was no sound. No wind, no birds, no hum of distant motors. Only the sound of snow falling, which was no sound at all.

52

It was so absolutely still that she could almost imagine she was dead. Only Tony's presence and the cold that was biting her cheeks told her otherwise. Tony had no such silly thoughts. "Shut the window," he ordered. "Cripes!" He was in a foul mood. He twisted around in the seat, stretching his legs and throwing out his arms. Cindy had to duck to avoid his feet.

She rolled up the window, at the same time becoming aware that the heater was blowing cold air into the car. "What's the matter? Why aren't we getting warm air?" She leaned forward to look at the various buttons and knobs on the instrument panel.

Tony swore under his breath. "We're out of gas!" He reached over the front seat to snap off the heater. "Keep the goddamn windows shut or we'll never stay warm till help comes."

Until help comes? She struggled to keep her imagination from running wild. *Think warm thoughts, Cindy. Buttered toast . . . steaming cocoa . . . a hot, hot bath . . .* But despite herself the car got colder by the minute. She was chilled right to the bone; her legs felt as if they were cast in ice. She could almost feel her lungs filling with ice and had to fight the choking feeling that took hold of her. She rubbed hard at her eyes, hiding her face against the stained, oily seat cushions. "What am I doing here?" she whispered. Who was she whispering to? Why hadn't she met someone older with sense and experience, someone like her father.

She reached out and turned the key in the ignition. Unexpectedly the car jerked forward, and there was a terrible scraping of metal. "Oh!" she cried.

"Damnit! You stupid jerk, what are you doing to my car?" Tony jumped forward. "It's in gear. Don't you know anything? Keep your hands off my car."

Cindy bit her lip and moved away. She had to do something beside sitting here and fighting with this boy. He didn't have a thought in his head but for his car and himself. She'd seen him admiring himself in the rearview mirror. He said they were going to be rescued, but she didn't trust him. He didn't know anything. Sit here and freeze to death? It was abysmally stupid. She had to get away, move, save herself.

She pulled her scarf around her head, got all her things together—books, the tin of cookies, and her denim bag. She started to get out of the car and then realized it was foolish to take the books. She dropped them on the seat. "I'm leaving my books here, if you don't mind."

"What are you talking about? Where are you going?"

"I'm getting out. I won't sit here and freeze to death. I have to do something." She tried the door. It was stuck.

"It's frozen shut," he said smugly. "You can't get out."

"I can!" She threw herself against the door, forcing it open against the snow. Outside it was gray and cold, and snow was still falling. The drifts around the car lay nearly level with the hood. It was a desolate scene—nothing but the snow and wind that whipped through the trees lining the hills. She would have slunk back into

54

the shelter of the car, but she couldn't face Tony's unbearable smugness. She began struggling up the slope.

In places the snow rose to Cindy's hips. She could barely move, but nevertheless pushed on across the field and up between the two hills, going back the way they'd come. Tony had called the hills Bear Hill and Slant Rock. The liar. He thought she would be taken in by his simple-minded lies. She knew they were lost. If she could get to a road, any road, she'd find her way to people and bring back help to him!

The going was terribly hard. Cindy floundered on, several times pitching forward to her knees and then struggling up again. She was covered with snow. It was in her eyes and in her mouth, and her boots were filled with it. She kept falling and picking herself up. The inside of her nostrils froze and her cheeks turned to glass. She thought of the satisfaction she'd feel leading people back to the car. Tony would still be inside admiring her conceited face in the mirror.

When Cindy finally gained the top of the rise and stood on level ground, she was panting for breath and sweating profusely. Wherever she looked, the snow, deep and glittery, spread in dazzling, windblown patterns. There was no road, no house, no chimney with its promise of smoky warmth. Only brush hills and the cold land rising and falling like waves in an ocean of snow. Looking back through the milky stillness, she saw the frosted outline of the car.

Her heart pumped furiously, the taste of salt was in her mouth. She felt sick and dizzy. In this huge, silent country she was only a tiny speck of life. She could feel herself dissolving like sugar in water. Disappearing . . . disappearing . . . Desperately, she ran forward, straight toward the horizon. Her scarf unraveled and flew off. Then she dropped her gloves, the denim bag, the tin of cookies. She lost everything as she struggled wildly through the snow. There had to be a road! "The road," she cried. "Where's the road? Oh, where's the road!"

Branches whipped against her face. She struggled through thick, bushy growths. Tree trunks loomed up in front of her. And then, tripped by some hidden obstacle, she fell face forward in the snow. She lay there, arms spread, her face buried. Slowly an uncertain calm returned to her. She remembered stories she'd read of people panicking in emergencies, losing everything as they ran mindlessly in circles, until they lost their strength and were truly lost.

She got up and retraced her zigzagging, crazy footsteps. As she came upon her things she picked them up. Her scarf, her gloves, the tin of cookies, and her denim bag. Each item she had dropped seemed to appear miraculously out of the whiteness like a sign post.

She smelled the car before she saw it, smelled oil and gasoline and metal, felt its presence the way an animal knows the presence of its mother. She stumbled forward gratefully.

7

SNOW BOUND

Tony HAD been watching out the window for Cindy, but when she came bursting back into the car, he was lying down with his feet over the front seat, a picture of relaxed indifference. Everything had gone exactly as he had expected.

"There's nothing up there," she said through chattering teeth. "Not a road, not a house, nothing."

"I told you not to go out, didn't I?" he said complacently.

"All right!" she said. "I don't want to hear about it now. My feet are wet and they hurt." Clumsily she pulled off her boots. "My socks are stuck to my skin," she said. "I think they're frozen. Oh!" She sounded ready to cry.

Tony leaned forward as she slowly peeled off her socks. Her feet were covered with purple splotches, but her toes were waxy. "Holy Mother," he said, "now you've done it. You've frostbitten your feet. You've got to rub them with snow quick or they'll rot off."

"You don't know what you're talking about!" she replied testily. "That's the worst thing to do." She'd taken a first aid course at the Y the previous summer. "This is nothing to fool around with." She warmed her toes with her hands. "Keep them dry and warm. Never massage the frostbitten area. Just around it. If you want to do something helpful, build a fire."

He stared at her. "A fire. Where?"

"Here," she said. "Where else?"

"Here! You mean inside? You're crazy," he said. "It'd ruin the car for good."

She wrapped her feet in her wool scarf and put her wet socks on the back of the seat to dry.

"How do they feel?" he said.

"How do you think they feel? Just leave me alone."

"Okay," he said. "Suit yourself." He lay with his legs tucked up under his chin and his hands between his thighs. That was the first and last time he was going to be nice to her. She just didn't appreciate anything.

It was cold. Gusts of wind rocked the car periodically, sending icy streams of snow filtering through the space between the windows and doors. Tony thought about stuffing paper into the cracks, but he didn't move, reluctant to leave his cocoon of body heat. He wished he could go to sleep and wake up at home in his own bed.

He could almost smell the ironed sheets his mother put on the bed every Friday. And food—he swallowed. He was hungry! Monday night they'd had pork chops and macaroni with butter and garlic, and the fresh crusty bread his mother picked up at Deloria's bakery on the way home. He and his sisters grabbed it so fast, the loaf was gone the minute his mother put it on the table.

Last night they must have been mad at him, thinking he was hiding someplace. But Tony was sure they'd be looking for him this morning. He twisted around to make himself more comfortable.

"I ought to have something warm to drink," Cindy said.

"Coming right up," he said. "Anything else?"

She didn't reply. That was fine with him. He could see her breath rising over the back of the seat. He heard her teeth chattering. A fire in the car! She was crazy. It wasn't her car. He was the one who would get it. Tony closed his eyes. Half dreaming, he saw the living room at home glowing with warm orange light, the color TV turned on to his favorite show, his little sister Evie lying on the rug, fanny in the air, reading the funnies. Maybe Flo was making a big bowl of buttered popcorn while Donna gabbed on the phone, shrieking and driving everyone nuts.

He had a lump in his throat. It was hard for him not to feel sorry for himself. He knew they were worried sick about him by now. He felt so sorry. He wished there was a phone he could walk to so he could call his parents and tell them he was all right.

He had been dozing, but he was wide-awake the moment his eyes opened. He felt uncomfortable, cramped, and icy cold. He rubbed his arms and legs hard. There was a leaden light coming in through the windows. At first he thought the snow had stopped, but it was only that a weak sun had pierced the dense clouds, shedding a pale, baleful light on the world. The snow continued to fall monotonously. They'd be buried before it stopped.

In the front seat Cindy was asleep, half sitting, half lying, with her feet wrapped in her scarf. Tony tried to roll down the window on his side. It was frozen tight. The same on the other side. He'd float away if he didn't get out and urinate, but he didn't relish facing the weather. Although the inside of the car was bitterly cold, at least they were protected from the wind.

Cindy woke. "Whaaa? Who is it?" she said in a startled tone. Her face was creased. She looked confused. She didn't wake up quickly the way he did, fast and ready to go.

"Your mouth was open," he said.

She turned away and wiped her mouth. Then she put her hand to her hair. She didn't speak. Instead she scraped a little ice from the window with her nail and peered out.

"How're your feet?" he said.

"All right," she said in a thick voice, and then in a monotonous undertone she said, "It might never stop. It could snow all day and all night, and tomorrow. We might never . . ." She didn't finish the sentence. Instead

60

she twisted around to look at Tony. "I got a little crazy this morning," she said, "when I ran out into the snow. But that won't happen again. It's important for us both to keep our heads and think. We have to cooperate. . . . We got into this mess and there's no use blaming anyone. Now we have to help each other. With some thought we ought to be able to get . . . to help ourselves. What do you think, Tony?"

"I think there's nothing to think about!" he said. "As soon as it lets up they're going to come through."

"Are you sure? What makes you so sure?"

"My father is looking for me right now!"

She shook her head. "What if he isn't? It doesn't have to be. Nothing has to be. We've got to help ourselves, that's the only thing we can be sure of."

Without answering he forced open the door. The way she was talking made him furious.

"Where are you going?" she said.

"To piss," he said. Let her think about that!

He went behind a tree to relieve himself. Then he stood absolutely still, listening. He stood for a long time, straining to hear distant sounds. There was nothing to hear, except the wind rattling through the trees. There was nothing to see. Nothing but snow and hills and snow-spattered dark evergreens. He couldn't see anything that looked like a road, but it had to be there. There was a road up there, he repeated doggedly. The snowplow was coming through. Help had to be coming.

Back in the car, he turned on the radio and they listened to the weather report from Watertown. A storm with blizzard-force winds had blasted the entire northern part of the state. Temperatures were in the teens. Five feet of snow had already fallen in Rochester, Buffalo, and Watertown. Drifts up to ten feet were reported in outlying areas. Schools were closed in every centralized school district. City schools were closed. Factories and stores were closed. Nothing was moving. Extra snowplows were being brought into the area to help clear the highways. Routes 20, 5, and 81 were closed. Dozens of travelers were stranded.

"People are advised to stay home," the announcer said. "Please, please, good people, don't travel unless absolutely necessary. All roads are in poor condition. Slippery, with blowing snow. Visibility near zero. Emergency situations should be called in to the police and sheriff's office. Fire and Civil Defense forces are standing by, and the road crews have been out all night plowing. The storm is expected to abate sometime this morning.

"So have fun, kiddies. No school today. Make some popcorn and stay warm and cozy around the fireplace if you have one, or the heater if you don't."

Tony clicked off the radio. There had been no mention of them, not a word. There was nobody looking for them. Nobody knew where they were. For the first time he truly felt despair. Their rescuers might never come.

8

FIRE!

"A fire," Cindy repeated. "We need a fire." Her feet were aching terribly. "We can't build a fire outside. The wind is too strong. Here at least, we have some protection."

He didn't reply. Biting and gnawing his nails like a dog, acting as if he hadn't heard a word she said, not responding. Waiting for his daddy to come and save him! It made her want to scream. How long could they sit here waiting for someone to find them? They'd freeze to death first. Oh, no, not her. She wasn't going to just sit there and turn into an ice cube.

Her feet were aching so badly that she could hardly think. "Fire!" she said again, rooting around in her carry-all. No telling what she had in there, it was so full of junk. She started throwing things on the seat. Wadded tissues, a nail file, an oval tortoiseshell lip gloss case, a half package of life savers. She'd forgotten them. Tony snatched them up. "You want any?" he said greedily.

"Take them." She held up a book of matches. "This is what I've been looking for! What fantastic luck." On the cover there was an advertisement for Rinaldi's Restaurant. "Dad and I ate supper there a couple weeks ago," she said. "We had chicken in a basket with French fries and carrot sticks." She was so excited she started to laugh. "Why did I take these matches? I don't smoke. I didn't even know I had them. Oh, how everything has meaning! What fantastic luck." She flipped open the cover. "Seven matches. That must mean something. But it doesn't matter, one match will start our fire."

"No fires," Tony said. "I told you, not in my car. Burn the inside of this car and my father will skin me alive."

"What's the matter with you," she exclaimed. "Your father wouldn't want you to freeze to death." She opened the glove compartment and rummaged through the things inside. A flashlight, tissues, road maps, two pencil stubs, a half-filled book of green stamps, a rusty beer can opener, a penny and a nickle, and a black wool mitten with the thumb missing.

Tony grabbed the stick of chewing gum. All he had on his mind was food. "That's my private property," he said, and swallowed the gum before he'd half finished the life savers.

"Your sense of values is distorted," Cindy said. "Private property means nothing now. I want to be warm. If we had one hundred dollar bills, I'd burn them." She threw the coins and the pencil stub back into the compartment and held up the road maps and the green stamp book. "We'll burn these. Now we need something to build a fire in. If I could only feel a little genuine heat again!" These last hours had been the worst of her life. She'd never been so cold and miserable.

"A fire will smoke up the car," Tony said.

Was he dense! Was he ever dense! "Will you stop worrying about your precious car and start worrying about us," she yelled. She was astonished to hear herself. "Our first duty is to survive, not to preserve the up-holstery of this car!"

"Okay, okay," he yelled back. He climbed into the back seat.

"We need something to build a fire in," she said. Where was he going now? "Don't waste your energy on frivolities. You've got to think fire."

He was kneeling, facing the rear of the car, yanking at the back seat, trying to pry up first one side and then the other. Cindy finally saw what he was doing—getting into the trunk from the inside of the car. "You want me to give you a hand?"

"No," he said, although the cold had obviously made him clumsy. He had to do things his own way. Her own hands felt like blocks of wood. Finally he freed the back cushions from the hangers and squeezed through to the trunk compartment. "The flashlight," he ordered. A moment later he threw out a green Army duffel bag with the name STAGNITTA stenciled on the outside in white. A brown wool Army blanket followed.

"Why didn't we think of this last night?" she said. "A real blanket!" She wrapped it around her legs and feet.

There was a gold mine of junk in the trunk. A pile of old newspapers, a length of clothes line, rags, a broken roller skate, a coke bottle, and an empty oil can. "Am I glad your people are squirrels," she said. "Tell me everything that's in there. I'll make a list. We should think about using everything." She watched as he stuffed newspapers and rags wherever he saw cracks of daylight. Then he backed into the car, passing her the empty oil can and a lug wrench. He stuffed more rags and papers around the doors and windows. "Did you find something for a fire?" she said.

He pointed to the oil can. "What do you think that's for?"

"It's so small . . ."

"You can't have a bonfire in here." After climbing back into the front seat, he put the can down between them on the floor and hammered on the top with the L-shaped lug wrench. He caught his fingers a couple of times, swearing and blowing on them before Cindy remembered the rusty beer can opener and handed it to him.

"What's this for?" he said.

She told him to use it to pry the rim loose before knocking it off with the wrench.

"Maybe," he said. But after he worked on the top, a single blow from the wrench tore it free. There was still some oil in the bottom of the can. Cindy ripped up one of the old road maps and twisted the pieces into tight spirals.

"Goodbye, Northeastern States, Maine, Massachusetts, Vermont, New Hampshire, and little Rhode Island. You're cold places, but you're going to warm us now."

Tony put the paper twists in place and struck a match. The match was soft and didn't catch. He struck it again and again. The whole book had gotten damp when she had gone rushing off into the snow and dropped everything.

"Here, let me," she said. She took the matches and drew one over the abrasive surface. Nothing happened. She struck match after match, but not one of them caught. A lump came into her throat. She wanted that fire as she had never wanted anything in her life. She gathered up the broken matches. Tony was biting his nails. "God," he said. Then their eyes met and almost in unison, they exclaimed, "The cigarette lighter!"

"The lighter works on batteries, and the batteries are still okay," he said. They had just been running the radio. He pushed the lighter in, then they waited breathlessly until it popped. Tony took it out at once. It was glowing a beautiful, hot orange.

"Wait a sec." Cindy held one of the matches to the glowing coil. The match caught; it was like magic. She held the match to the paper twists. The fire flared in the oil can, yellow, acrid, smoky, but with a little glow of heat that sent them both huddling close. They had made a fire.

9

ISLAND IN
THE SNOW

CINDY TOOK a tin box out of her carry-all and shook it. "And now supper," she said. Tony had seen the tin before, but thought it contained some kind of personal stuff, maybe a sewing kit. It sounded like buttons. Cindy carefully pried open the cover, revealing mounds of chocolate chip cookies.

Tony's mouth watered. "Cookies! You had them all the time, didn't you? And I've been starving. I bet you've been sneaking them!"

"I haven't touched them!" Cindy's eyes became flinty and she pushed his arm away. "We're sharing. We're going to make these cookies last." She pushed them into little piles, counting. "There are forty-eight cookies. Twenty-four for you, twenty-four for me. Six each tonight, six each tomorrow night."

"That only makes twenty-four," Tony said.

"I'm making provision for two breakfasts, just to be on the safe side. Six tonight, six tomorrow morning, six tomorrow night, six the next morning—"

"What are you, a computer," he yelled. He pushed her hand away and dug into the cookies.

"How many did you take?" Cindy cried. "Eight! Then you have sixteen left, that's all. If you want to be a pig . . ." She took four cookies, clamped the cover shut, and put the box on her side away from him. "We should be sharing everything," she said. "Fifty-fifty. Helping each other. That's why I saved the cookies. If I hadn't we wouldn't have anything now."

"Don't give me any of your speeches," he muttered. Always preaching. The lady preacher. It was hard for him not to feel guilty. But he wasn't surrendering the cookies.

He was starved. In an agony of desire he immediately shoved two of the sweet-tasting rounds into his mouth. Down they went, soft, sweet, and dark. Nothing had ever tasted so good. He tried to make the other six last a little longer, but he couldn't stop himself from gobbling every one. When he had none left, Cindy was still nibbling at her second cookie. Out of the corner of his eye he saw the way she took a tiny little bite, her mouth and throat working slowly, then another tiny little bite. It was driving him crazy.

"What are you looking at?" she said, catching him watching her.

"Nothing." He turned and cracked open the window on top to clear some of the smoke. Then he lifted the back seat again and hauled in the rest of the newspapers. Under the pile he discovered half a dried up peanut butter sandwich. He pocketed it stealthily.

They took turns warming their hands and feet over the fire. The smoke made their eyes water and often sent them into fits of coughing. They both worked at twisting the newspaper into tight spirals. The fire had to be fed continually. They'd soon need wood. Through the window Tony could see the dark line of trees at the edge of the field. He'd get wood if this damn snow ever stopped.

From time to time he broke off bits of the peanut butter sandwich in his pocket and sneaked them into his mouth. He was hollow, hungrier than she was. She was chubby, didn't need food as much as he did. He had to eat. The bread was gritty, hard, and tasteless, but along with the cookies it began to fill the aching emptiness inside him.

They crouched over the fire, watching the ice thicken on the inside of the window. Outside, the snow fell relentlessly. The wind shook the car. The fire took the chill off the interior—but barely. From time to time Tony rubbed his arms or legs. Cindy had her feet wrapped inside the green Army bag and she offered to share foot room with him. "It really helps," she said. His impulse was to refuse, to say he was just fine the way he was, but his feet had been stone cold ever since the engine stopped.

So they sat close together, their feet in the sack, the blanket over their shoulders. Tony despised sitting cramped this way, so near her, but he *was* warmer. Already he could feel some of the cold and stiffness leaving his arms and legs. Only his face felt the nip of the cold. He could smell her hair and the lip gloss she had smeared over her face to protect it from the cold.

He thought of his mother. When he was little, he and his sisters used to get into bed between his mother and his father. Tony would usually be on his father's side, but sometimes he'd be next to his mother. He could smell her warm skin, feel her softness. She'd wrap him in her arms and rub her cheek next to his, kissing his neck till he couldn't stop giggling.

Time passed slowly. Tony eyed the cookie tin on Cindy's side. Her socks dangled from the dashboard over the oil can fire, slowly steaming dry. His boots were tipped up near hers on the floor. When he moved, she warned him not to hit her feet.

"You think *your* feet hurt," he said. "I went hunting with my father last fall and I thought my feet were coming off. Man! My father and my Uncle Leonard, they're so crazy for hunting they wouldn't go back to the car to warm up for nothing! So *I* couldn't go back. We were out for geese. It was raining and cold. I mean *cold!* We drove up somewhere around here and went into this farmer's cut-down corn field; and just as we were walking into the field, a whole flock of these

Canadian geese went honking up in the air. My father and my uncle were knocking off their shots, going crazy, shooting as fast as they could. The geese were screaming and honking and flapping around. Most of them flew off, but a couple of dumb clucks kept circling us. They didn't have brains enough to get away."

"And you killed them?" she said.

"Of course we killed them. That was the point. We gave them to this guy Fred Fields, because he has a freezer, and my mother can't stand cleaning birds. Mrs. Fields said she'd make a roast goose dinner for everyone this winter. She hasn't done it yet. Man, I'd like some of that goose right now."

"I don't understand," Cindy said. "Why would anyone want to kill animals or birds? Animals are so beautiful and perfect in themselves. They don't harm anyone. Not geese. Maybe some of them are a little nuisance to the farmer, but they do good, too, eating bugs and things. Why do you torment them? Why can't you let them live in peace."

"You like to eat, don't you?" he said scornfully. Men had always been hunters, right from the beginning, while women had stayed home. She could never understand the feeling of getting up before dawn, dressing quickly, gulping scalding coffee, being jammed in the station wagon with his father and the other men. The rough jokes, the heft of the gun in his hands, the sack of sandwiches they shared, and the thermos of hot, sweetened coffee, and then the thrill and scariness of the geese flying up, honking so madly in a frenzy to escape. Man, that was living!

72

Dusk fell, and with it the wind died down completely. For long periods they were quiet, listening. The only noise was a crow in the distance, sounding like a rusty door hinge.

When the snow stopped falling they both became aware of it at almost the same moment. "It's stopped," Cindy said. "It's really stopped!"

Tony whooped. "Only one more night! Tomorrow we're going to be out of here."

Cindy looked over at him with an expression of joy on her face.

"It'll be like a bad dream," she said.

10

WHERE WERE THE PEOPLE?

IN THE FADING light a crow appeared, black and feathered, its ragged wings blotting the evening sky. "He's beautiful," Cindy said.

"They'll be coming now," Tony said. "Now that the snow has stopped, someone will come looking for us. By morning, sure." His breath came in little white spurts.

"Smoke signals," Cindy said, making her breath puff the same way. "Frozen words. Maybe somebody will see them, like secret messengers. Did you ever wonder, Tony, what happens to the words you speak? Where do they go after you say them? If you could know how they travel, you could direct them to anyone

74

in the world. Hello out there, world! We're here! Come and get us!"

Her voice echoed off the dark hills. Both of them listened intently for an answering sound. "Yell again," Tony said excitedly. "I think I hear something."

They called together. "Hell-ooooo out there! Hello-oooo!" Each time, Cindy told herself that this time somebody would hear them. They called until it grew dark and their voices were hoarse. They kept the window open longer than they should have.

"This is futile," Cindy said, shivering. Tony rolled up the window, leaving it open a crack on top. It seemed incredible that nobody answered. Where were the people? Even though they had such high hopes for the next day, the prospect of another night in the car was depressing. They talked about the problems of keeping the fire alive through the night. If they both fell asleep, it would certainly go out. And how long would their paper fuel last? Already they were using the last of the newspaper for their miniature logs, which burned up shockingly fast. Cindy said if it came to that, she'd gladly burn her books. "My geometry book first."

"I'm going out and see if I can find some wood," Tony said.

"In the dark?"

"You ought to get out of this car, too," he said. "You've got to move, keep your circulation going."

"How can I, with my feet this way?" She could barely put her weight on them.

"Don't you even have to answer nature's call?" he said.

"I have the constitution of a camel."

Tony rolled down the back window on his side and rolled out of the car, head first. She watched as he made a path through the snow, until he disappeared against the darkness of the woods. Despite the cold, she kept the window wide open, listening for the sound of snapping wood. Not seeing Tony, she felt uneasy. "Tony? You okay?" she called.

He returned carrying an armful of dead branches that he pushed through the back window. "I'm going for evergreens now," he said. "For bedding."

This time when he returned with his arms loaded, he pushed the fragrant green boughs into the front on her side. Then he climbed back into the car himself. "I'm frozen." He peeled off his gloves to warm his hands around the fire can. "The fire's out!" he said indignantly. "You were supposed to keep it going."

She'd completely forgotten the fire. "Tony, your hands . . . I'm sorry!" It was a terrible thing to do. Hurriedly she pushed in the cigarette lighter. Tony held his hands around the can, then stuck his fingers into the ashes.

"Cold," he said, and threw the ashes into the snow.

Cindy tore a piece of paper out of her geometry book and twisted it tightly. "The sum of the square of the hypotenuse . . ." Tony stared at her balefully. "Only being cheerful," she said. "Adding a little gaiety to the proceedings." His disgusted look made her feel

76

like an idiot. She concentrated on the cigarette lighter. The paper smoldered against the orange coils. It was damp, but it finally flared up.

"That battery isn't going to last forever," Tony said.

Cindy fed in twigs, and the fire smoldered. The wood was wet and greasy. "This wood's not very good." She bent over the can, blowing gently on the fire. Her hands were cupped around the edge, feeding pages torn from her book. "We need a knife to cut shavings. Shavings would take."

Tony tried shredding a branch with the beer can opener. The nail file Cindy offered him worked a little better. "We'll get it going now," she said. She laid twigs across the top of the can to dry out, and worked on peeling another branch with her fingers. She held up her stumpy nails. "Now I wish I had sharp fingernails."

After a while they had a small pile of wood chips and slivers of bark, but when she put them on the burning paper the fire still sputtered weakly. "Don't go out, don't go out," she whispered. "You can have my English book, whatever you want, beautiful fire. Stay with us, please little fire." At Tony's astonished look, she said, "I'm praying to the spirit of the fire."

"You take the prize. You better watch out, or the little men from the funny farm will come to take you away."

"Don't you have any reverence? Any religious feeling?" She blew on the fire. It was taking now.

"For a fire!"

"Yes, for a fire. Why not for a fire? It means life, doesn't it? The sun is fire. Without it, where would we be? I mean human beings, and all life on earth."

"You're way too deep for me," he said sarcastically.

When the fire was burning, they arranged themselves in the front seat for sleeping. First they spread the evergreens like a carpet on the floor. The greens smelled wonderful and kept out some of the cold. Then they put their feet into the Army bag again. Cindy's were still terribly tender and achy, and she warned Tony not to jar them.

"You told me a million times already," he said.

Sitting side by side, they pulled the blanket around behind them and brought it around to meet in front, where, with a safety pin Cindy had found in her jacket, she pinned it together like a shawl.

It was dark inside the car. The long night stretched before them. Only the tiny fire under their feet gave off a shadowy yellow light. Neither of them slept. They were too uncomfortable. "We ought to talk about things," she said. "Get our minds off ourselves. Do you have a girl friend?" Tony shook his head. "I bet girls like you. You know, you're very handsome. No, you really are. I go to school with a boy who looks something like you. He's Italian, too—do you mind my mentioning your ethnic origins?"

"Why don't you stop trying to impress me?" he said. "All those five-dollar words. What's wrong with saying things plain?"

She didn't think she was being artificial or offensive.

"That's just the way I talk," she said. "I didn't mean to offend you." Stiff, she thought to herself. She sounded stiff as ice. Why couldn't she say things easily and naturally, the way she felt.

"Tony," she whispered a little later. "Are you sleeping?"

He grunted and bent forward to feed the fire. Every time he moved she had to move, too. "I can't sleep," she said. "Do you want me to read your palm?"

"I don't believe in that junk."

"It's just something to do to pass the time." She took his hand and held it close to the light of the fire. "Look at the lines. What do you see?"

"I see the number forty-one backward on my right hand, and forward on my left. What does that mean?"

"That's not the way you do it." She showed him the mounts under each finger: Jupiter for ambition under his index finger, Saturn for seriousness under his middle finger, then Apollo for brilliance, and Mercury for practicality.

"Where'd you learn that?" he said.

"I was reading a book." She showed him the Mount of Venus at the base of his thumb. "That's your love mount."

"Stupid," he said, but he was interested as she showed him his head line, his heart line, and his lifeline running from the base of his wrist to just under his first finger. "What does this stuff mean? What does it show?"

"You're going to have a long life," she told him, "and several unhappy love affairs."

He pulled his hand away. "Cripes, what baloney." But a moment later she saw him studying his palm. "Too bad you can't tell when we're getting out of this mess," he said. "Then your fortune telling would be worth something."

11

THE HELICOPTER

When he was sure that Cindy was finally asleep, Tony moved stealthily, unpinning the blanket, and reaching over her to lift her denim carry-all to his side. "Quiet," he told himself, "quiet as a cat." He got out the cookie tin and slowly pried off the cover. Saliva gathered in the corners of his mouth. Crazy, her holding the cookies out on him, he thought. And him so hungry he could eat a horse.

He took a handful of cookies, not counting, telling himself they were his, anyway. Easing the cover back, he put the tin into the denim bag, which he placed back on Cindy's other side, and then he pinned the blanket together with a smile of satisfaction. He ate the cookies one at a time, slowly now, having learned that from her, letting the taste collect in the back of his mouth, then slide smoothly down his throat.

The next morning Tony heard a noise and woke up immediately. He'd been dreaming about his father showing him the moisture under the distributor cap. "That's the reason the car wouldn't start," his father said. Tony awoke hearing engines in his head. Was the car engine running?

Outside, he heard the clatter of an engine cutting the air. The next moment he had kicked free of the blanket and was rolling out the back window with Cindy just coming awake behind him, crying, "What is— What? What's happened?"

"It's a helicopter," he yelled, and he stumbled, fell in the snow, picked himself up, ran toward the sound waving his arms, yelling, "Here! Here! Here we are!" looking toward the sky, yelling hoarsely, dimly aware of Cindy behind him with the car window rolled down, crying, "Help us. Oh, please help us, please, please . . ."

But already the sound was disappearing, the clatter of the engine receding and echoing over the hill. "I never even saw it," Cindy said. "I only heard the motor. I never even saw it."

Tony waited outside, stomping his feet, praying the helicopter would circle back, listening for the clacking, clapping noise. He searched the gray sky until his eyes watered, but there was nothing. The aircraft had disappeared. No noise, only the raucous cries of blue jays calling to each other in the woods. He felt sick with disappointment.

Cindy was watching from the car's open window. "They must have been looking for people stranded in the storm. We need a signal—maybe a fire—to guide them next time." She told Tony how the car had looked from the hill, half buried in the snow. "From the air it must look like nothing more than a bump on a log."

She was right about that. He followed his path to the edge of the trees and began dragging branches and fallen limbs to make a pile in the middle of the field. If they came again, he'd push a rag into the gas tank and then light it under the wood. That way they'd get a smoke signal up fast.

Finally he climbed back ito the car. He was freezing and needed to warm up. Cindy was working on the fire. "You know something else we ought to do?" she said. "Stamp out the word 'HELP' in the snow."

Something else for *him* to do later. She had the ideas, but he did the work. He rubbed his hands over the fire. He'd run out without gloves and with his boots only half laced. She could go next time.

"What would you like for breakfast this morning, sir?" Cindy asked jokingly. "Scrambled eggs? French toast? I make really superb French toast, crisp and brown on the edges, soft in the middle."

"Cut it out. I don't even want to think about food." His belly felt hollow, scooped out like an empty cup.

She opened the cookie tin, started to count out cookies, frowned, and stopped. She'd combed her hair till it stood out around her head like a halo. She looked at Tony, then back into the box. "You took cookies," she said. "When did you do that?"

"I only took what was mine."

"How many did you take this time?"

"I didn't count. I was hungry, so I ate some. What's the point of hoarding them?"

Her eyes flashed. "You're a fool." She took out a few cookies, closed the box, and put it away. "You've eaten more than your share. You stole mine."

He ignored her. While she ate, his stomach growled and churned. To show her that he didn't give a damn he chewed ferociously on a sliver of wood.

Later, Cindy said she had to get out of the car. Tony watched as she gingerly pulled her socks over her swollen feet. They still looked puffy and awful. Her face was white as she tried to stuff her feet into her boots.

"Here. Take mine," he said. He pulled off his boots and shoved them toward her. They were a couple of sizes larger than hers, and she was able to get her feet into them. While she was gone, he rummaged in her denim bag, and then opened the cookie tin and ate a few more cookies. He could have eaten all of them. He snapped the box shut and pushed it away.

After that he occupied himself turning her nail file into a knife. He used two pieces of wood and some copper wire he'd unwound from the old generator in the trunk. When Cindy returned he held up the homemade knife. "Maybe I can get us a bird or a squirrel with this."

"How do you think of these things?" she said.

"I don't *think* of them," he said, mocking her. "I just do them." Later, he got out of the car and sharpened

84

the knife on a flat stone—spat and ground the edge, spat and ground again. He tried the knife out, hurling it at a squirrel in the crotch of a tree. The squirrel went chattering away and the knife sank uselessly into the snow. Tony retrieved it, and afraid to lose it, decided not to try again.

All through the morning, both of them listened and watched. The helicopter didn't return. Instead, around noon snow began falling again. Not heavily, but enough to cover the wood Tony had piled in the field, and the top of the car he had so carefully cleared in the hope that when the helicopter returned it would notice the shine of the roof. The rescuers should have been here by now. He'd been listening for them for hours and they hadn't come. The longer he waited the more desperate and impatient he became. How did he know they'd ever return?

"Can you walk?" he asked Cindy.

He knew the answer even before he asked. He'd heard her crying outside earlier as she hobbled toward the trees to take care of herself, and she'd come back nearly all the way on her knees. He bent over to feed the fire. They had to do something. They couldn't just sit around here for another day with almost nothing to eat, waiting for rescuers who might never come. It was up to him. He had to get help for them. She couldn't walk, so he'd have to go alone.

"No! We're better off together," she said when he told her. "When you're lost you should stick together, and stay in one place."

"Sure, if someone's out looking for you, it's good

advice," he said. "But who's looking for us? I mean, who knows we're here? You said it yourself! That helicopter checked this section and he's not coming back." He couldn't sit in the car any longer and freeze and be hungry and let things happen to him without doing something. He'd go crazy this way. His idea was to get up there on the level ground and then keep going, plowing along, leaving signs as he went until he got out of this place. There had to be people somewhere nearby. He'd find them. He had to find them, didn't he? This was New York State, not the wilds of Alaska.

"What direction will you take?" she asked. "How will you know to get back here and find me again?"

"I'll leave signs," he said.

"Will you come back as soon as you can?"

"As soon as I get help. Maybe I'll come back on a snowmobile. Or in a helicopter." He wanted to leave at once. He laced up his boots, stuck the knife in his belt, and was ready to go.

Cindy took off her long red-and-black plaid scarf and gave it to him to wrap around his face. "For when the wind starts blowing," she said. She opened the cookie tin. She said nothing about the extra cookies he'd eaten, but gave him nearly all that remained, leaving herself only a few.

"They're yours," he said, although he couldn't keep his mouth from watering. "I had mine."

"You'll need the energy. Go on, take them." Her eyes were filling, getting larger and shining, swimming with lights, like water with the sun's light on it. He stuffed the cookies into his pocket. He looked around the car. She had a nice pile of twigs in the back seat to feed the fire, and the blanket and Army bag to keep her warm. She only had to sit inside and wait. It was up to him to get help.

"Maybe I'll be back tonight," he told her. "Maybe I'll find help right away. I'll be back before you know it." He went out through the window, striking out eagerly up the hill.

12

A HANDFUL OF CHOCOLATE CHIP COOKIES

As CINDY watched Tony plow up the hill the sun came out, making her eyes water. At the top of the hill Tony stopped, turned, and looked back. "Good luck, good luck," she called. She shut her eyes against the sun, and when she looked again he was gone.

For a while she stayed by the open window, listening, forgetting the fire, sometimes holding her breath with the hope that almost at once Tony would spot a road or a house. Then he'd be coming back, whooping triumphantly, and they'd laugh hysterically together over their stupidity—to have been so close to rescue all this time!

The wind was blowing icy particles against her face. Reluctantly she rolled the window up almost to the top. She fed the fire from her store of twigs and sticks. Greedy, how greedy the fire was, licking everything up, like a bright hot lollipop.

She dozed off for a while, waking to see the sun slanting through the windshield. The wind came gusting across the field, splattering snow against the car. Cindy rubbed her legs and changed position. She nibbled a cookie, ignoring her stomach's clamoring.

I'll be thin when this is over. I'll never have to diet again. She imagined herself back in school—the questions, the comments. How had she changed from a size fourteen to a petite eight? "My secret," she'd tell them, "was four days on a handful of chocolate chip cookies. You, too, can do it. Any brand of cookie will work the same magic."

The wind moaned. Was there someone else trapped nearby, crying for help? The trees swayed and bent, and the white drifts piled up in scalloped dunes like sand at the shore. Her father had taken her to the shore the summer she was twelve. That was the same summer he bought her a camera, and every time he pointed to something beautiful—a sunset, whitecaps, a flight of gulls in the air—she had taken a picture of it.

She formed her hands into a rectangle before her face, squinted one eye. Click! "Lucky me!" Another candid shot of this beautiful nature scene for her album.

Mother Nature, what a lie! She remembered how she had always loved to walk alone on foggy evenings with the light funneling around the street lamps. She'd lift her face to breathe in the wet softness of the air. She indiscriminately loved fogs and first snowfalls, thunder-

storms, winds of thirty miles an hour, and hailstones—
the bigger the better. She loved the first leaves in the
spring, the sticky sap on pine trees, the sound of pigeons
flapping over the roofs like wet laundry on the line. She
thought it all meant something. Could all this beauty be
without meaning? In the past she'd said she didn't believe in God; neither did her father. She'd always felt
that Nature was God. What a lie! Beautiful Nature was
cruel and indifferent. God, at least, whatever he was,
cared.

*I've decided to keep a kind of journal, not really a
diary, just writing things down as they occur to
me. This is my second day alone. I found the little
green spiral notebook that I use in school for assign-
ments and stuff. Too small to make much difference
to my fire.*

*When Tony comes back maybe I'll talk to
him about some of the things I've been thinking.*

*In the afternooon: clouds of dusty snow funnel
around the car, the wind racing across the open
field.*

*My foot aches and aches. My face in the car
mirror sooty, strange, wild. I don't recognize myself.
There was a smell in the car like burning wool.
I've singed my hair.*

*My second night alone. I don't dare fall asleep
for fear the fire will go out. I'm keeping the fire
higher, which smokes up the car terribly. Tony's*

*poor car! If I open the window any wider I'll freeze.
Between the smoke and the cold and a hacking
cough that has lodged in my chest I never fall into
a deep sleep. Little cat naps. My neck stiff. Waking
scared. Listening.*

*Short hooting sounds. Owls? They could be
dogs barking. Even horses whinnying.*

*My third day alone. I think it's Saturday,
though it might be Sunday. It bothers me that I can't
remember. It was Tuesday we were wrecked. We
were together Wednesday, and Thursday Tony
left. So it's Saturday. I feel I've been alone forever.*

*Am I starving? I've hardly eaten, but I don't
feel the least bit hungry anymore, only thirsty. I eat
snow and can't stop shivering.*

*Where is Tony? What if he's lost, wandering
in circles, and will never come back. Stop it, Cindy.
Stop that kind of backward thinking!*

*I saw a deer today. I don't think he saw me. He
came out of the woods at the foot of the hill. He
looked so thin and scruffy. He was nibbling something in the bushes warily, raising his head and
listening with those big ears, and gentle eyes. If
Tony had seen him, he'd have wished for a gun.*

*I've always hated waiting for anything or any-
one. Waiting for Tony to return is the most difficut
waiting I've ever done in my life. Lots harder than*

*waiting in a dentist's office, or waiting for Dad to
come home at night. I keep looking, expecting that
the next moment I'll see Tony coming over the hill.*

*Just looked again, probably for the hundredth
time. Nothing. No one. Not a sound. Even the wind
has died down.*

*It's strange how you change your mind about
people. Take Tony and me. At home I would never
have looked twice at a boy like him. Never would
have thought about him, or wondered what sort of
person he really was. Boys like Tony are all over,
a little too conceited, a little too good-looking, a
little too know-it-all. They always know better than
any girl! So spoke Cindy, the people pigeon-holer.
But right now, I freely admit I've never waited for
anyone the way I'm waiting for Tony. And it's not
only the selfish longing to be rescued from this awful
place. I really want to see him. I try not to think
about it, but I'm scared for him. He's been gone so
long.*

*Stupid feet. If I hadn't panicked and run off that
first morning and gotten my feet frostbitten. If I'd
been a little more careful. If I'd sat tight in the bus
station.*

*Isn't that the way everyone talks? If, if, if. If ifs
and ands were pots and pans, there'd be no need for
tinkers. That was in my nursery rhyme book when I
was a baby, but it's still true. The important thing,
as my father would say, is to do things right the first*

time. But that has to be impossible. I can't help leaping ahead and being frustrated, and then thinking about what's past and being sorry.

I blame myself now that Tony and I weren't friendlier. I'm so quick to feel injury—to find fault, to see the worst side of people. I should have tried harder.

I think my feet are actually getting better. I can touch my left foot without wincing. The puffiness is definitely down. Right foot still sensitive, but better.

It's getting dark. I've been writing in this notebook on and off all day. I write a little and then look up, feed the fire, doze, watch out the window, write some more. I dread another storm, Tony lost in it, his tracks obliterated, myself buried in this metal tomb. Oh, shut up, Cindy!

I'm sipping hot tea. Doesn't that sound elegant? I crook my little finger— tea is so refined. But really it's only hot water, and it tastes wonderful. It may be the best thing I ever drank in my life. This is how I got it. Eating snow isn't very satisfactory as a thirst quencher. First of all it freezes the inside of my mouth before it melts, and then it starts me shivering, and I noticed I got cramps when I took down too much too fast.

If only I had something hot to drink! I thought. It seemed like the most impossible wish in the world.

Then—I don't know why—I thought of the ashtray in the dashboard. I pulled it out. Full of cigarette butts and gum wrappers. I dumped the cigarettes, but saved the gum wrappers, then wiped the inside of the ashtray with my shirt. I dipped fresh snow into the ashtray through the window, put a stick through the little bar across the top and balanced it over my fire.

I had a tea kettle! I felt as thrilled as Fulton must have when his steam engine worked. Even so, the first few times I melted snow in it, it still tasted of cigarettes. Ugh. I had to dump it out and boil away again. Finally, success! Hot water with a little spearmint gum flavoring. What could be better? My belly is full of hot water, beautiful hot water.

13

THE DESERTED LANDS

AFTER LEAVING the car, Tony didn't look back until he had climbed to level ground. Then a quick glance showed the roof of the car below, like a blue plastic bubble. Hesitation gripped him. The bare hills rolled in every direction with not a sign of human life anywhere. Now he had to choose. Forward, or back. Forward—how long before he found someone? What if he never did? But when he thought of going back to the car, he imagined Cindy laughing at him scornfully, calling him a coward.

He turned slowly, memorizing the dip in the land, the black-and-white scratchy hills rising on all sides, and higher than anything else, the wide-armed branches of a giant oak.

He started off. With each step he floundered knee deep into snow, soft and heavy as mud. It was an effort to lift his foot and take the next awkward step. And then another. And another. By the time he'd gone fifty feet he was beginning to sweat. He looked back. Already the car had disappeared from view. Would he be able to find his way back? He looked to the giant oak for reassurance. The wind nipped his face. He readjusted and knotted Cindy's scarf more tightly around his head. Slowly he continued trudging forward.

It was hard work, the hardest he'd ever done. He had to stop frequently to get his breath. The sullen gray sky slowly changed to broken clouds. The trees, black against the snow, also changed color, the aspens glowing like gold. Tony stopped often to look around, note some landmark, break a branch as a marker. He knew there were dirt roads, cow paths, old logging trails crisscrossing all through these hills. The thought that he would come out to a real road made his heart leap and gave him the strength to keep going. His thoughts kept flying ahead to the snug farmhouse with smoke rising from the chimney . . . or the farmer's red pick-up truck . . . or the line of telephone poles he'd follow.

Onward and upward, his steps slogged along to that phrase. Onward and onward. He trudged doggedly forward. But when he turned and saw behind him the crooked, disordered line of footprints disappearing in the snow, something curdled in his stomach and a sinking feeling took hold of him. In the back of his mind was a fear he wouldn't admit, that nightmare he sometimes had of being pursued down a dark, reverberating tunnel . . . running along dark corridors, faster and faster, opening doors to empty rooms that went on and on and led nowhere.

He forced his attention to a bare rock face on the hill behind him. "That's a rock face," he told himself. And before that there was the split pine, and before that the big oak. He noted shapes of trees, and rocks, and made markers that would help him retrace his steps.

It must have been a mile to the top of the rise. Breathing hard and hot, Tony estimated that the mile, which under ordinary circumstances he could walk in fifteen minutes, had taken him over two hours. He wiped his forehead. He'd had to fight the snow every step of the way, but now he was at the top. He looked around expectantly. Before him lay a plateau covered with snow, clumps of woods, and more snow. There was no cozy house, no barns, no road of any sort. No sign of people or animals. Nothing to direct him. Only the desolation of trees and snow everywhere, as if this were a million years back in time, and he the first and only man on earth.

"Hell-ooo," he yelled. "Helll-ooooo!" His voice echoed back to him, lonely and uncertain.

He was cold. His feet, which had ached for so long, were now without feeling. He thought of stopping and longed for a fire, but he was afraid of falling asleep in the snow, afraid of losing time, afraid of not getting across this barren sea of snow.

He planned ahead. "I'll walk across to those evergreens." There seemed to be a road between the trees, as if the area had been reforested. But when he got to the trees, there was nothing but more snow and trees.

The afternoon dragged on. Several times Tony leaned against the trunks of trees, taking shelter from the wind for a few moments, then moving on. He was having a truly incredible adventure, he thought to himself. When it was all over, his family would be impressed. He'd persevered. He'd gotten through. He had done something nobody else had done.

"Tony . . . my wonderful boy." His mother's voice was warm in his ears. She put her arms around him and cried tears of joy. "That poor girl would have died without you," his mother said. "You saved her. You're a hero, a real hero." His sisters danced around, wanting to hug him. And his father . . . his father . . . why, his father would clap him on the back, take him to the shop to show him off to his buddies. "What happened to the car was an unforeseen accident," he would say. "It could have happened to anyone. If it had happened to me, I couldn't have done better than my boy."

He was dreaming, his hands deep in his pockets, stepping, sinking, feet rising clumsily to step and sink again. He was almost asleep on his feet. The voices, the admiring voices, the applause, rose in volume. "You walked all that way, kid . . . in the snow!" "You really are something!" "Hey, you can say *that* again." "What a kid!" "Nobody else could have done it, I'll tell you. . . ."

A flight of chickadees landed in a tree ahead of him. Their cries woke him. "Dee, dee, dee!" they whistled cheerfully. Little black-and-white birds cutting in and out like miniature acrobats. He pulled the knife from his belt and flung it at the birds. He lost his balance and pitched forward in the snow. He rose clumsily to his feet. He'd missed by a mile. What good were chickadees anyway—a mouthful of feathers and tiny bones. His stomach growled. He nibbled red berries from a bush and spat them out. So bitter, he thought he'd been poisoned. He spat again and again, scraped bark from a pine, chewing the wood to kill the bitterness.

Tony picked up his knife under the tree. Behind him he saw his tracks staggering and twisting through the snow. Where had he been? Where was he going? He was alone in a way he'd never been alone before in his life. Around him in every direction he was crowded by trees. Trees behind him, trees ahead of him, trees on either side. All thought of a road was gone. He plunged forward between the trees, where the snow was thinner. Ahead of him he saw a house and a barn. He was saved! He ran forward, shouting at the top of his lungs. "Hello! Hello!" But when he drew closer the house and barn turned out to be the long shadows of trees against the snow.

He went on. He saw fires and buildings, people waving to him in the distance. But it was always in his mind. The fire of the sinking sun, a white tree with strangely human branches, or the snow whipped up into what seemed to be little outbuildings.

He didn't know where he was. He didn't know where Cindy was. A terrible feeling gripped him. He was lost. He ran blindly, howling at the top of his lungs.

Finally he made himself stop. He stood still, breathing hard, grasping the scaly orange trunk of a pine and rubbing his face against it. He bit his icy fingers through his mittens. It was stupid to go on this way. Hopeless. The sun was going down. A blue chalkiness filled the air. He had to find shelter for the night.

He burrowed into the protective darkness of a low-branching spruce. A grouse flew up with a loud squawk. Tony made a clumsy dive for the bird and regretfully watched it disappear into the trees. It was damp and earthy under the spruce, but he was out of the wind. Tearing branches from the tree, he spread them on the ground to make a bed and blanket.

He blew on his fingers, flexing them, blowing, working them together until the feeling flowed like fire and they hurt so much that he had to put them under his arms and hold them there. His feet were throbbing, and darts of pain came and went in his legs and back. He curled up in the boughs, and despite the cold and the aches in his body, he fell asleep.

Tony dreamed about the dog and food. He saw himself in front of the open refrigerator at home. Every time he took something out, the dog snatched it out of his hand. "Down, boy." He was worried that if his mother saw the dog sniffing in the refrigerator she'd have a fit. He popped a piece of juicy steak into his own mouth. Nothing had ever tasted so good. The dog was jumping up, begging for some, but Tony had to have another piece for himself first. The dog kept jumping and trying to get into the refrigerator. "Stop that," Tony said, and woke up to hear the echo of a dog's bark.

It came again, loud and chilling. Stiff, aching, he pulled himself up, fumbling for his knife. Barking again, and then that icy howling. His skin crawled. Wolves? Or wild dogs?

He'd heard plenty of stories about the packs of wild dogs that roamed these deserted lands, tearing live deer apart, savage, untamable. Tony remained still, hairs prickling along his neck, the knife gripped in his hand. He strained his eyes to see through the dark, interwoven branches. They were out there, he was sure.

Suddenly he yelled. "Aaa-eee!" Again. And again, until his throat ached and his whole body was throbbing.

After that, he couldn't sleep. He squatted, hands between his legs, listening until the sun came up, rimming the sky with washes of pink. He rolled out from under the tree and stretched and jumped. He found a heavy, solid stick to use in case the wild dogs were still around. Their tracks circled the tree, the prints in the snow appearing enormous.

Tony struck out with the sun at his back. He was hungry. His jaw ached, his legs ached, every bone in his body ached. He'd keep going west until the sun was overhead, and then he'd rest. If he hadn't found anything by then, he'd turn back.

As he moved along he talked to himself. He was going to find something, somebody—soon. He was lucky. He'd always been lucky. Look at the stories his family told about him. All the times he'd wandered away from home when he was really little. His parents scolded and yelled, but he'd always found his way home all right. Nothing had ever happened to him. God wouldn't let anything bad happen to him. His father didn't go to church, but Tony still went with his mother and sisters, so God knew about him. God wouldn't forget him.

Tony talked to God: "If you're watching me right now, if you get me through . . . I'll be one hundred percent in every way from now on . . . no swearing, no picking on my sisters, no hitting . . . one-hundred-percent cooperation with my parents."

But God had to get him through to someplace, safe. He wouldn't go back on his word. The Lord could count on that. "Help me, and I'll be good forever," he said out loud.

He nearly stumbled into the stream. Bright, moving water in the snow. A piece of luck. Really good luck! A change in the landscape. Streams went from high places to low places; people lived near streams; animals drank from them. This stream had to lead somewhere. Tony decided to follow it.

14

NIGHT CREATURES

*My third night alone. Not sleeping much. Afraid my
fire will go out. It's only me and my fire now. Cold,
clear night—the snow blue. If I live here a hundred
years I'll never get used to this awful quiet.*

*Woke with a start. I've been dozing. What if I
fall asleep and never wake? Freeze to death.*
*Fed my little fire twice as much as necessary.
I'll live as long as I have my fire. Feel like a cave
woman crouched before her hearth, full of super-
stitious dread.*

*Felt depressed and began composing farewell
notes to everyone I love. Dad. Grandma. All the kids*

*I knew. I think of you all now. I used to be so criti-
cal of people and life—everything. I never gave anyone a chance to get close to me. I had to be so aloof,
so critical and demanding.*

*Have to stop every couple of words and warm
my fingers. I'm shivering all the time.*

*The pain and discomfort I'm experiencing now
must be for some purpose. I can't believe that I'm
going to die. My life has hardly begun.*

*I'm going to live and be a better person. I have
to have that chance.*

*Yesterday I saw three crows sitting on a tree. I
felt their black, beady eyes on me. What were they
waiting for?*

*I just woke thinking I was dead. Then I felt the
cold.*

*If my thoughts turn to death again I'm going to
make a noise in my throat, chrrrrrr, and scare Death
off.*

*The silence hums. Beneath it, I hear all kinds of
strange noises. Little animals, night creatures tunnel-
ing under the snow—mice and moles, and God knows
what else. My heart, too, thumping away in terror.*

*The night makes everything strange. Woods are
closer, and the hills hang over the car. I begin to
imagine the ground sliding out from under me. The
wind crackling through the frozen bushes sounds like
the clicking bones of dead people. I almost hear them
tiptoeing up to the car.*

"*Who's there?*" *I actually yelled out loud. The sound of my own voice frightened me more than any noises. I had to laugh at myself. Happy Ghouls' Day, Cindy!*

But I still locked every door from the inside. As if that would stop those skinny-boned ghouls. They slip through cracks.

Where is Tony? I keep looking for him. Surely by now he's found someone, something, someplace. The worst ideas go through my mind. I can't help remembering how greedily he grabbed everything. What if he's found help and forgotten me. Tony, you better come back!

Just before dawn I fell asleep, long enough for my fire to go out. Stupid! I shook the fire can. Barely warm. Not a spark left, and it was cold again in the car. First mad at myself, then anxious, then remembered the cigarette lighter. Not to worry.

I pushed it in and waited calmly. Tore out the last sheets of my geometry book and rolled them up. Got my twigs ready. When the lighter didn't pop, I pulled it out. The coils were cold. Puzzled, I pushed it in again, waited, meanwhile inspecting my feet. They seemed one hundred percent better, but I needed the fire. I'd die without the fire.

Again I had to pull out the lighter. Cold and dead. This time I thought to turn on the radio. That, too, was dead. The battery was dead. I didn't stand a chance without fire. Already I felt the cold creeping into the car.

I asked myself what I should do. I remembered the bonfire we'd planned to make if the helicopter returned. We were going to use a gasoline-soaked rag. What I had to do, then, was get some gasoline on a rag, then try to get a spark out of one of those limp book matches I'd saved. A spark and gasoline.

I pulled on my boots and crawled out of the car. My right foot still hurt when I put too much weight on it. A long stick wasn't hard to find, and I ripped a piece of upholstery to tie on the end. Tony would have a fit.

The gas tank cover was frozen and wouldn't give to my efforts to unscrew it. I dug around in the snow for a rock and banged away at the cap until it broke loose. I pushed the stick down the neck of the tank as far as it would go. I came up with nothing. Too short.

I followed the path to the woods, found a longer stick and attached my rag again. A simple movement, but it took the longest time. My hands were stiff as ice. I seemed to have ten wooden thumbs. But it was done finally, and again I pushed the stick down into the gas tank. I swished it around, and when I pulled it up I didn't have to sniff to know the rag was soaked.

In the car again, I put the soaked rag in the fire can, said a little prayer to fire and wood, and struck one of the paper matches. Nothing happened. My heart sank. I was so cold. I studied the matchbook,

*looking for the driest, roughest place. Doing every-
thing slowly and deliberately. I held the match and
booklet next to the rag, said another prayer to sparks
and fire, and struck down again.*

*The fire exploded out of the can, throwing me
back, singeing my face. Thick, acrid black smoke
filled the car. But when I saw the yellow flame I for-
got my stinging face and fed paper and then twigs
until the fire held steady. I warmed first my hands
and then my feet, and then my hands again.*

*Now that my fire is going again, hunger has sud-
denly returned to torment me. I'm ready to eat bark
from trees. Not a bad idea?*

*Found this poem in my English book. By Chris-
tina Rossetti. I memorized it easily before I burned it.*

> *In the bleak mid-winter*
> *Frosty wind made moan*
> *Earth stood hard as iron*
> *Water like a stone;*
> *Snow had fallen, snow on snow*
> *Snow on snow,*
> *In the bleak mid-winter,*
> *Long ago.*

15

COLD BEANS
FROM A CAN

THE HUT stood on a knoll across the stream Tony had
been following. A dark, weather-stained structure, with
a steep tarpapered roof. Tony crashed across the stream
and up the other side, yelling with excitement. No one
answered his call. No smoke rose from the chimney, and
as he approached he saw that the windows were boarded
shut and the door padlocked.

The cabin was empty. A terrible anger gripped him.
Anger at whoever owned the cabin for not being here.
He pounded on the door. Tears smarted his eyes. To
have come all this way for nothing! And now his feet
were wet, too—his boots soaked through. His feet
would freeze! Enraged, he picked up a rock and ham-

mered at the lock, battering it until the hasp tore loose and the door swung open.

It was dark inside and even colder than outdoors—a chill, numbing cold that made Tony's head ache. He was in an uninsulated hunting-and-fishing camp of the cheapest construction, probably used only in milder weather. There were chairs stacked on a table, a couple of cot mattresses folded double on bare metal springs, and a stuffed duffel bag on the floor. A half-filled wood-box stood behind a squat old fashioned black stove. On a shelf Tony found a book of wood matches—sturdy, dry matches that struck bright and true the first time. He threw kindling into the stove, opened the draft, watched the strips of wood catch, then added more and more wood as the fire roared up. Nothing in his life had ever looked or felt so good. He shut the front door, threw more wood on the fire, pulled off his wet boots and socks, and collapsed on one of the bare mattresses.

Hours later he woke to the sound of hammering. Still groggy, he thought it was his mother calling him to get ready for school. He didn't want to get up. He was cold and shivery. He felt horrible. Why didn't she leave him alone?

He sat up, looking dazedly around the dark cabin. The cabin. Of course, he was in the cabin. Was it night already? Then he remembered the boarded windows that he hadn't had the strength to open. He stumbled to his feet. "Who's there?" The hammering stopped, then started again. He pulled open the door, half expecting to see the wrathful owner of the cabin. No one was there.

The countryside spread before him, pale, blank, and ferocious. The hammering had begun again, this time on the other side of the hut, and he realized that it was only a woodpecker probing beneath the bark slab sides for hibernating bugs.

Tony built up the fire again, then looked carefully around the cabin. It was an ordinary hunting and fishing camp, but he examined each object in it as if it were made of gold and jewels. A wooden shelf between the studs of one wall held a candle stuck in an empty beer bottle, a jelly glass, and a battered teapot. On the front of a high wooden cupboard door was a faded calendar with a picture of a fisherman in hip boots smiling proudly at a trout glistening on the end of his line, while behind him a waiting bear was smiling too.

In the cupboard Tony found a yellow canister with seven teabags, a large glass jar filled with rice, a salt shaker, a full bottle of ketchup, two cans of beans, a can of tomatoes, a can of corned beef, and a green glass jar filled with sugar. His mouth watering, he dipped a handful of sugar and almost gagged on the sudden rush of sweetness to his stomach. He knocked the chairs off the table and spread all the food from the cupboard in splendid array. In a dark corner of the cupboard he found two spongy, sprouting potatoes that he added to his hoard. He was dizzy with his wealth. He wanted to devour everything at once.

He decided on a steaming bowl of beans and searched for a can opener, swallowing his saliva. He yanked out the drawer in the kitchen table. Everything clattered to the floor. He was slow and clumsy with hunger and fatigue. There was a real knife, a few forks, a spoon and corkscrew, but no can opener. He flew into a rage and kicked the chair. He couldn't control himself.

He filled the tea kettle with snow, put it on top of the stove and poked up the fire. He'd soon need more wood, but he dreaded the thought of going out in the snow. Instead, he took one of the wooden kitchen chairs and bashed it against the wall until it splintered and came apart in his hands. He fed the chair into the fire. After the water in the tea kettle had boiled, he threw in handfuls of rice and shook in ketchup freely. The spicy smell was dizzying. He licked the rim of the ketchup bottle and carefully capped it. While the rice was cooking, he investigated the duffel bag. It was full of blankets.

When his meal was cooked he gobbled the rice and ketchup, scraping out the bottom of the pot, then licking his fingers clean. To keep the fire going he broke up another chair. Then he slept under seven blankets.

In the morning the fire was out and the hut cold, so Tony stayed under the blankets dreaming about snaring a rabbit and roasting it over the fire. Reluctantly his thoughts shifted to Cindy and the return trip. Those fields of snow. Sinking down to his hips. He could almost feel it all again like a physical presence, an enemy punching and battering him, dragging him down until he didn't know or care where he was or what happened to him.

Outside, the sky was slate gray. It had begun snowing again. What was the use of going out and getting lost in a snowstorm? Wouldn't it be better if he stayed here and waited for someone to show up? Then he could lead them to Cindy. They'd both be better off waiting in different places. He'd been gone two days now. Cindy had as good a chance of being rescued as he did, maybe better. Maybe somebody had already come for her, and his return trip would be entirely wasted.

Yes, he'd stay here a while longer. There must be fish in the brook. He could burn the rest of the chairs and then the boards on the windows. After that, there was plenty of dead wood around.

Later he found a few bits of string and tied them together to make one long piece. He didn't need a lot of line, only enough to get into the water. He used a bent safety pin as a hook, and baited it with a small piece of potato sprout.

He used the outhouse, then went down to the stream, looking for a pool where he could let down his line. Snow was falling. He found a flat rock, cleared a place for himself, and squatting down, dropped his line slowly into the water. He could see the baited hook sinking down like a white worm.

At first nothing happened. He waited impatiently, hunkered down, his legs slowly turning bone cold, the falling snow stinging his bare neck. A small fish flashed toward the bait. It sniffed, nibbled, and then before it could spit the bait out, Tony snatched up the line and hooked it in the gills. A small five-inch trout. There were several more near misses, but finally he landed another fingerling, and three shiny, dark suckers.

In the cabin he cut each little fish in half, cleaned it, then skewered them one by one on the knife, broiling first one side then the other over the fire. He ate all of them down to the bones, including the heads. Then he licked his fingers and went to sleep.

As soon as he awoke the next morning, his eyes fell on Cindy's scarf lying across the bottom of the mattress. Cindy's scarf. She'd given it to him before he left and he'd worn it around his head on the whole trip.

He threw himself out of bed, angered and irritated. He broke up the last kitchen chair for the fire and then hammered open a can of beans. He ate the beans cold from the can, scooping them up with his fingers. Cindy the Lady would give him a lecture on that. Cindy.

"I'm coming, I'm coming," he said. "Don't worry so much, I'm coming!"

But he put it off one more day. He couldn't resist the lure of the cot, the seven blankets, the heat of the fire, and the mushy, spicy taste of fish, rice, and ketchup. That rice and ketchup! He could have gone on eating that for the rest of his life and been happy.

That night, before going to sleep, he made his preparations for the return journey. He packed sugar and tea, and the three remaining cans of food into a blanket roll. He made straps for the roll by cutting the plastic tablecloth into strips, which he tied around the blanket and under his armpits. He'd found a pair of gray wool socks with holes in the heels, and he stuffed these in a side pocket of his jacket. Then he lay down to sleep. In the morning he'd start back.

16

RED WINTER BIRD

WHEN CINDY saw Tony coming down the hill late Monday afternoon, his face flaming, a crazy pack on his shoulders, and her scarf knotted under his chin, she thought at first she was hallucinating. She'd waited to see him for so many days that now she didn't believe it. She watched him come closer and closer, getting bigger and bigger, and still she didn't make a sign. And then he was banging on the locked car door, and she rolled down the window, feeling her face split in a tremendous smile.

Tony came sliding into the car, shivering and stamping. She grabbed him, meaning to kiss him, but he turned his face and the kiss landed on his ear. Never mind. He was here! She wasn't alone anymore. He'd only found a deserted hut at the edge of a stream, but she was too happy to have him back to be disappointed.

"I thought you would have been rescued by now," he said.

"Nobody came."

"We'll go back to the hut tomorrow," he said. "We'll take whatever we can from the car." His eyes darted around impatiently. "Boy, this car—what a mess! Can you walk okay now?"

That was her good news. "Do you think I was sitting in the car all the time you were gone?" She pointed to the wood she'd gathered, told him how she'd restarted the fire, and the way she'd learned to make hot water. She was eager to share her experiences. "My feet are much better, and now that you're back, if I had a teabag and a spoonful of sugar, life would be really sweet!"

Like a genie, Tony reached into his jacket pocket and produced a tea bag and a little plastic sack of sugar. Immediately, Cindy boiled snow in the ashtray on top of the oil can. She dipped the teabag in the boiling water just long enough to color it. Then she carefully added a pinch of sugar.

"Put in more," Tony said. "Go on, don't be so stingy. There's plenty where that came from."

From the way he described the camp it sounded as if he'd discovered Aladdin's cave. "Mattresses and blankets, and the stove is half the size of this car. Hey, did I tell you there's an outhouse?"

"An outhouse. What luxury! Tell me again what's in the cupboard," she said. She put a bit more sugar into the tea. She wanted to conserve everything. They still weren't rescued.

They took turns sharing the tea, eating slivers of cold corned beef from the can. "This must be the greatest gastronomical experience of my life," Cindy said.

"You and your five dollar words," Tony said. "You haven't changed."

She looked at him seriously. "But I have, Tony. Those days alone . . ." They had to make a person different. "I've changed a lot." Now, she thought, was the time to share her notebook.

"You want any more corned beef?" he said.

She had the notebook open in her lap, but Tony showed so little interest that she finally put it away. It didn't mean that much, she told herself, but she was disappointed.

Later that night they each had a blanket to wrap themselves in. Tony was asleep almost instantly. She listened to him breathing in the back seat. They had agreed to alternate sleeping and watching the fire, but he was exhausted and sleeping so soundly that she didn't bother waking him for his turn. It was easier for her. She was used to the routine of napping and waking.

In the morning it was snowing again, and the wind was blowing fiercely. The clouds were low and heavy, and the interior of the car was filled with gloom. Tony opened his eyes, looked out the window, then shut them again. "You look awful," she said.

"I don't feel so hot." He cracked the window to peer outside, letting in a blast of snow. "Snow! I hate it," he muttered.

He slept all day while Cindy kept watch on the fire.

He woke several times, each time saying they'd start for the cabin in a little while, each time falling asleep almost immediately. Toward evening the snowfall stopped, and a weak trickle of sun came through the clouds. Cindy went out and brought in a load of wood. Her feet were in good shape now. Thinking about the trip to the cabin she jumped up and down to get in condition. Suddenly a scrap of red in a tree caught her eye. It was a red cardinal, slender and proud, tail working. He was vivid, almost unreal against the white landscape. She took a step toward him, a question on her lips. She wanted to know how he kept himself so beautiful in all this desolation. But he rose into the air, dipped, and disappeared.

It was dark when Tony woke up again. He said he felt better. She handed him a container of hot water and a slice of corned beef. "I was dreaming," he told her. "I was home and we were having supper. My sisters were there, and my Uncle Leonard. My mother passed me the hamburgers and my sister Evie gave me her orange soda." He swallowed. "I want to get out of this place. I want to go home."

They looked at each other. What could she say? Home. The very word made her eyes prickle with tears. It was a week and a day since they'd gone off the road. In all that time, nobody had come. She had stopped believing that anyone was looking for them—at least not in the right places. Now she only wanted to hang on, to keep her strength so she'd be alive when they finally came.

17

YELLOW SNOWMOBILES

IN THE MORNING Tony was impatient to go. It was a perfect blue, icy day. He went outside and began yanking on the hood of the car. He pried at the hinges with the lug wrench. The car didn't matter anymore. He was sick of the car, sick of the smoky fire and the cramped life. They were walking away today and not coming back. Sweat sprang out on his forehead and he tired quickly. "What I need is a crowbar," he grunted. Cindy found a rock and began banging on the hinges.

As the sun climbed higher in the sky, Tony's initial good humor faded. He hated the car. It was fighting him, holding him back. When the hood didn't come off easily he was ready to bash it in, destroy it totally. Finally one hinge snapped, and then with both of them

118

twisting on the hood, the other hinge bent and gave. Breathing hard, they flipped the hood over into the snow. The rounded front end rose like the prow of a toboggan. Tony attached a long piece of rope to it and the sled was ready to go.

They gathered everything of value from the car. The flashlight, knife, can opener and lug wrench all went into the green duffel bag. They took the blankets, their ash-tray kettle, and the fire can, which they'd keep alive on the way. For insurance Tony soaked some rags in the last of the gasoline in the tank and stored them in the empty cookie tin.

Everything was piled onto the sled. "Let's go," Tony said.

"It's like leaving home." Cindy was peering into the blackened interior of the car. "It looks so empty and ruined."

"Come on," Tony urged. The wrecked car gave him a bellyache. He had the rope over his shoulder and was pulling the sled.

"One minute," said Cindy.

Breathing impatiently over her shoulder, Tony waited while she wrote a note. "We waited for you more than a week and you didn't come. We're trying to get back to a hunting camp Tony found. Maybe two or three miles from here going west, near a brook. Please come soon. We're hungry and cold and don't know how much longer we can hold out." She printed their names on the bottom, and then they both signed to make it official.

Tony inserted the note under the horn ring inside

the car and then shoved the keys under the sun visor. The last thing they did was clear the snow off the roof. It was later than Tony had meant to start, but they were on their way.

His old trail had been obliterated by the new fall of snow, but at the moment he wasn't worried. He'd snapped branches, so there were landmarks. With the sun at their back, the direction was generally westward.

At first the climb went well—not fast, because they were plowing through deep snow, but they were moving steadily. Behind him, he could hear the steady crunch of Cindy's steps like the sound the dentist made tamping silver into a tooth. He did most of the sled hauling, but she took her turn, and when it got stuck she was right there to push.

Showing off a little, Tony pointed to animal tracks that crossed their path. "Rabbit," he said at the arrangement of two short and two long tracks. "Fox." He pointed to an arrow-straight track. Deer were easy and so were bird tracks. As they plodded on there were other tracks that weren't so good, big padded prints. Dog prints. "Wild dogs. They run in packs." He told her about the night he'd slept under the spruce tree, and she looked queasy.

"Do you think they would have attacked you?"

"Animals are afraid of people," he said.

The climb was wearying. They stopped talking. At the top of a rise, Cindy said, "I have to sit down," and dropped onto the sled. Tony leaned against a tree. He was cold and uncomfortable.

"Which way now?" Cindy asked.

He saw the slashed pine and a familiar rock face. "That way." He pointed west. He was no longer so sure of the way he'd gone before, but it seemed right. There was no use saying anything else. "I see signs," he said definitely, immediately swallowing the little anxiety he felt.

The sound of the snowmobiles seemed to be coming from all around them, growing louder and louder so Tony thought that any second the machines would burst through the woods into sight. "Here!" he shouted. "Here we are!"

But almost as quickly as the sounds had come up they began to fade. Tony knew they hadn't been seen. Their cries hadn't been heard. Nobody could hear anything over the noise of those machines.

For a long time they stood listening, as long as the faintest drone of the motors could be heard. Of all the rotten luck. People—rescuers—had been so close, and they hadn't been seen. The cabin was forgotten. They had to reach the snowmobilers. Find the snowmobile tracks and follow them. They were so close to being rescued. "Hurry," Tony said. "Hurry." They set off at once, Tony's eyes fixed on the spot where he thought he'd seen the yellow machines.

"Wait for me," Cindy called. She was dragging behind him.

"Can't you go any faster? What's the matter with you?"

"My feet hurt," she called back.

He muttered to himself. She was always slowing him down. Right from the beginning she'd been bad luck.

Ahead of them was a long, sloping decline. When they reached the bottom they would be almost at the woods through which the snowmobiles had disappeared. It was Tony's idea that they get on the sled and ride it down the long slope. Cindy was reluctant, but Tony wasn't listening. "We have to move. Do you want to catch those people, or don't you?"

The ride started beautifully, with Tony kneeling in front holding the lock and Cindy behind him gripping the rope. The sled moved slowly at first, but gradually it picked up speed, moving faster and faster until they were racing down the hill like an arrow. Tony laughed exultantly as the wind whistled against his face. Trees and rocks whipped by, his eyes stung with excited tears. Now they were moving! They were going to be saved! "Saved!" he shouted.

"Too fast," Cindy screamed in his ear. He laughed derisively, but a moment later they were going so fast that there was no stopping or controlling the sled. He tried to turn it with his body. The sled glanced off some rocks, then spun around and kept on its mad course, Tony barely aware that Cindy had been thrown off.

The ride ended suddenly and disastrously, as Tony shot through a line of thin bushes and over the edge of a steep ravine, the sled flying out from under him in midair. For a moment he was flying, too, trees and bushes below him, and then with a sickening thud he hit the ground.

Above him he heard Cindy calling, yelling his name. He started to pull himself up, thinking he'd only had the wind knocked out of him, but when he tried to stand, his left leg buckled and he fell back. The dread that had been growing in him from the beginning, when he'd wrecked his mother's car and they'd been marooned in the snow, now overwhelmed him. It had all come to this. His leg was broken. He couldn't go on. There was no way in the world that they'd be saved now.

18

TOO YOUNG TO DIE

CINDY LAY in the snow where she'd been thrown, deep, deep in the snow. She closed her eyes against the hateful white all around her, trying not to think, wishing she could go to sleep and never wake up. She didn't know what had happened to Tony. She was afraid to look. She ached everywhere. She lay there, letting herself sink into the enormous white stillness.

Oh, my God, God, God, God. Oh, my God.

Get up, Cindy.

She squeezed her eyes shut. No, she'd never get up.

Get up! Up! Move!

Leave me alone . . . I'm tired . . . so tired . . .

Cindy Reichert, get up. On your feet. Right now. Reluctantly, unwillingly, she struggled to her feet.

Snow was in her eyes and in her mouth and down the back of her neck. Carefully she made her way down the slope where Tony had disappeared. He was at the bottom of a deep, brushy ravine. She slipped and slid down the embankment, grabbing bushes to slow her descent. Tony was sitting in the snow, holding his leg. The sled and the equipment were strewn all around him. Why didn't he get up? "Tony," she called. "Tony, are you all right?" He didn't move. He acted deaf and dumb. What was the matter with him?

"Tony—"

When she got to him she saw that he was crying. "Tony, what is it?" He hid his face. It was too awful, seeing him with his head bent and his hand over his face. "Oh, Tony, what happened? Tell me, are you hurt? Where did you hurt yourself?"

"It's my ankle. I think it's sprained or broken." He rubbed his eyes, then forced a smile, but his expression was fearful.

If Tony couldn't walk, they couldn't move. It was the worst thing that could have happened. They'd been through so much already. Too much. Cold and hunger, out in this awful snow and desolation for days and nights. Now this. Stuck here in the middle of nowhere without shelter or food, they'd freeze to death. Why were these things happening to them?

She had to stop her thoughts. She was close to panic. She forced her mind to turn to practical matters: getting Tony out of the snow, making a fire, fixing a shelter. His teeth were chattering. She didn't feel much better, but at least she could move. She found the blankets and the rest of their things in the snow. She wrapped a blanket around Tony's shoulders, turned the sled right side up and helped him onto it. He was shaking badly.

"Let me see your ankle," she said.

He didn't want her to touch it, even look at it. "It's all right. Leave it alone!" Just by looking at the way he held it she knew it wasn't all right. She made him roll up his pants leg. Then she worked off his boot as carefully as she could. He swore under his breath.

Something was seriously wrong with his left ankle. The bones didn't look right. The ankle, bruised, was already swelling. When she touched it he winced. "Damn it! Leave me alone."

"All right," she said, "don't be such a baby!" She felt nervous and fearful. She didn't want to touch his ankle again, but she couldn't leave it the way it was. Everything she'd learned in first aid the previous summer came up a blank. She remembered that she had to wrap a fracture or a break and keep it as motionless as possible. She straightened up, looking around for sticks for a splint. Then she tore strips from the blanket and wrapped his ankle as best she could. Tony sighed and moaned and bit back tears. She was sorry. "I can't help it, Tony. I'm trying to be careful." At last the job was done.

He was weak from the accident, maybe suffering from shock. He needed warmth. Cindy kept talking, fighting despair. "Okay, we've got that under control. Your ankle's going to be okay now. I think it's just sprained. Not broken, that's not so serious, is it? Now let's see if we can get you on your feet." If they were to get out of this place, he had to walk. She couldn't carry him! She found a heavy stick caught in the crotch of a tree. "Here, you can use this stick as a cane," she said.

"I can't," he said. "I can't stand."

"Sure you can," she said, forcing a cheerful tone into her voice. "Go on, try it. I can't carry you. You have to do it. Get up, Tony, you have to walk."

Steadying himself with the stick, he gingerly put his weight on his injured leg. "Good," she said, "that's very good!" But at the first twinge of pain he threw out his arms and sank down on the sled. "I can't! I told you I can't!"

Cindy looked up at the steep sides of the ravine. She had never felt so afraid and hopeless in her life. If he couldn't stand, they couldn't move. If they couldn't move, they would freeze to death—that was the truth. A chill shook her. They had to move. They couldn't stay like this. They had to find fire and shelter.

Some distance away, jutting out from the side of the ravine, Cindy found an outcropping of rocks that formed a narrow shelter. "There," she said, pointing it out to Tony. "We'll go there and build a fire." He nodded, indifferent to everything but his own misery. She had to pull him on the sled while he sat there like a dead weight. She threw herself against the rope. The sled barely inched along. It was terribly hard work, but she finally made it across to the rocks.

When she recovered her strength, she scooped out a place between the rocks. Then she went to work on a fire, piling dead branches high and putting the gasoline-soaked rag underneath. "Pray," she said as she struck the match. The fire flared up. She threw in more wood and soon had a roaring fire that heated up the shelter. Then she lay down next to Tony on the sled and pulled the blankets over them. She was tired, so terribly tired, too tired to think.

Later, she got up and gathered firewood and springy evergreens for bedding. They ate the last of their food, a can of tomatoes. Tomorrow there would be nothing.

Tony was propped with his legs toward the fire and his back against the rock. "My whole leg hurts," he said. "It aches and aches. It doesn't stop aching."

It was hard for her not to feel resentful. She hurt, too. Her body throbbed, her head throbbed, she thought she had a fever. Every time she looked at those steep ravine walls, she got a sick feeling in her stomach.

Tony snapped off twigs and flipped them into the fire. He had stopped shivering, but he was still depressed. "We'll never get out of here. We're going to die here."

"No, we won't." Her words were hollow. She didn't believe them. She was as depressed as Tony. She didn't want to hear anything anymore.

It was growing dark out. Her eyes felt rimmed with sand. She put the green bag around their legs, one blanket over that, and another over their shoulders. She dropped off to sleep at once.

Hours later, she awoke, confused and coughing, her jaw aching from being pressed into her shoulder. The fire was smoldering, the smoke streaming right into their shelter. Next to her, Tony was asleep half sitting up, and moaning from time to time. Cindy threw wood on the fire. Beyond the rim of the fire it was pitch dark, but almost at once she sensed something or someone out there. The hairs on the back of her neck bristled.

"Tony," she whispered. He woke at once, listening and alert. He sensed it, too. There was something out there, something dark and menacing, watching them.

Cindy reached for a heavy stick. Then, on the shadowy edge of the fire, she saw a dog emerge from the darkness, and beyond him the long muzzle and glassy eyes of another dog, and then still another. Her first reaction was relief. They looked so friendly. The first dog was sitting on his haunches, his tongue out. There must have been half a dozen of them around the fire.

"Dogs," she said, thinking they were pets who had wandered away from a nearby farm. "Tony, we must be near someplace. They can lead us to people! Here, boy," she cried, getting to her knees.

Tony yanked her back. "Are you crazy? Those are wild dogs."

She shrank back against the stones. Hearing Tony's voice the dogs shifted their positions, moving slightly back beyond the light of the fire. But the leader, the one in front, remained where he was, yellow-eyed and un-blinking.

"Don't touch them," Tony said. "They're hungry and wild. They're unpredictable." He picked up a rock.

Cindy threw more wood on the fire, spreading the circle of light. The dogs backed away. Now she could see they weren't family pets. Their coats were matted, long, and filthy. Wild dogs, with sharp, gleaming teeth, like wolves. She built the fire higher. When she looked again, they had left without a sound.

Neither she nor Tony slept much after that. Twice during the night they heard the dogs howling in the distance. Afterward, in the silence, they listened tensely, ears straining for the least sound.

Once Tony said, "I wonder what happens when you die."

"We're not going to die," she said sharply. "We're too young to die. We're getting out of this place. We'll find a way. We have to. It would be too stupid to die here because I stuck out my thumb, and you took a wrong turn."

As soon as it was light, Cindy retied the bandages on Tony's ankle.

"Jesus, damn it! Leave me alone! Quit!"

"It has to be tight," she snapped. Tony looked terrible, his eyes dark, his lips cracked from the cold. Neither of them had slept much. They were both irritable. The sooner they got moving, the better. The dog tracks were thick at the edge of their shelter. It was stupid staying here. Moving, they had some hope.

There was no way to go but down through the ravine. Tony sat on the sled while Cindy pulled. Before she had pulled a dozen steps she knew she hated the sled. She tried pulling first with one hand and then with the other, and for a while she tugged backwards with both hands. Tony helped by pushing with his stick, but it was so rocky in the ravine that every few feet the sled stalled.

Each time it happened, Tony swore and complained bitterly about his ankle hurting. They had to stop often to rest. Cindy felt weak and sick. She wanted to cry. Her hands, even with her gloves, were swollen, stiff, and cracked from the cold, and torn raw from pulling the sled. Her lips felt thick and scabby, her head swollen and pounding. If only she could believe that they were truly coming out somewhere, but they seemed to be going deeper and deeper into this awful wilderness.

Several times she thought she saw the dogs. She couldn't free herself from the fear that the dogs were stalking them, waiting for an opportunity to attack. Once she saw two dogs outlined on the edge of the ravine above them. Another time she was sure she saw the leader watching them from a big rock, but when they drew closer it turned out to be only a stump.

They struggled through the ravine for hours, a lifetime to Cindy. She was sweating, sore, exhausted. All her pulling and yanking seemed to be getting them almost nowhere. As time passed and absolutely nothing changed, she grew more and more depressed. Why were they going on this way? Why this pain? What had they done to deserve it? There was no answer. Fear drove her ahead. If they stopped now they might never find the strength again to move.

Above her, a frosted sun, white through the clouds, rose higher. She felt as if she'd been pulling on the rope forever. Tug and fall, and tug again. No beginning. No ending. Nothing but tug and fall, tug and fall, over and over.

And then, like a black snake sliding under the rocks

and ice, a stream appeared. Tony said streams were meant to be followed. That was how he'd found the cabin. The stream filled them both with hope, gave Cindy the strength to pull again. *Please, Stream, lead us somewhere . . . to a river . . . a house . . . to people . . . oh, please, please . . .*

They followed the water as it twisted and turned beneath the ice and rocks, until it disappeared into a frozen swamp. Withered cattails, tufts of frozen grass, and a forest of swaying dead black trees. All was deathly still except for a woodpecker rat-tat-tatting somewhere high on a hollow trunk. Dismay and disappointment lumped sourly in Cindy's throat. Which way now? They couldn't go ahead. Left or right—it was all one. They didn't know where they were, or where they were going.

Tony's head was sunk down on his chest. It was useless talking to him. Cindy circled the sled, swallowing down the panic, trying to think. There were tracks in the snow, the round dog pads she recognized now, and near them the sharp wedgelike deer tracks. Under an uprooted tree she found a hollow where the deer must have rested. Then, shockingly, a stain of bright blood in the snow.

She stood for a time, held there by the blood. She imagined the deer, its terrified flight from the ravenous wild dogs. Its blood was as real to her as her own blood. Sickened, she took up the sled rope again. "We've got to go on, we can't stop here." Tony waved his hand limply as if he didn't care about anything anymore. She tried to drag the sled alone, but it was impossible if he didn't cooperate. "Tony, come on, push. We're not staying here."

"I don't care. Leave me alone," he said. "Just leave me alone."

"Then start pushing," she ordered. "Those dogs are somewhere around here." The way his head sagged down between his shoulders, she was afraid he'd never move. "Lets go, Tony. Push!" He sat there as if he were deaf and dumb. It scared her. "Do you hear me? I said the dogs are here. They're after a deer. They could be after us. Are you coming, or do I go alone?" Her feet were freezing in her boots. She could feel them aching right up to her hips. A dead tree creaked mournfully. She hated this place. "Are you coming?" she screamed. "Or do I go alone? I mean it!"

He raised his head and smiled cruelly. "Go on. Who's keeping you? Go any way you want to. I don't care. Don't hang around me. I'm sick of you! If I didn't pick you up, I wouldn't be in this trouble. I was safe in the cabin and then I came back for you. You're bad luck. Go away and leave me alone. I'll get along by myself!"

It was too much for her. She was too tired, too cold, too aching, scared, and miserable to take any more of this. If he felt that way, then she didn' care either. She grabbed her carry-all, wrapped a blanket around her shoulders and walked blindly away.

She hated Tony. She hated him! He had ruined everything from the beginning, stupidly getting them lost, thinking only of himself, taking chances they couldn't afford. The sled ride that had ended in disaster—that had been the stupidest thing of all!

Talking to herself, she plodded farther and farther on until Tony was out of sight. Now she was alone in the woods. She was glad. She was free of him. She could move. She had a chance to save herself. She stopped and looked back. Clouds again obscured the sky. A sharp wind sprang up. The air was raw against her skin. She hitched the blanket tighter around her shoulders. Snow had begun to fall. Grimly she plodded on. In a few minutes she'd be separated from him forever. Already she didn't see or hear anything but the wind high in the trees. She listened to the terrible silence. Alone. She was alone, terribly alone. Without Tony, she felt doubly alone.

All along, in the back of her mind, she'd been aware of how stupid and ridiculous their fight was. They were both so tired, hurt, and exhausted that neither of them could think straight. This was the time they needed each other most. Together they had a small chance of being saved. Alone they were both lost.

She had turned and was retracing her steps when she heard Tony yell in the distance, a desperate inarticulate cry for help. Cindy dropped everything she was carrying and ran, floundering through the snow. As she broke through the trees she saw Tony on the ground kicking and backing away from a pack of snapping dogs. It was a vivid, horrible sight. Screaming, she ran forward as the lead dog, jaws bristling, rose in the air, froze for a moment like a black sail, and then came crashing down at Tony's feet. "Tony," she screamed. It was then she saw a small deer lying half dead in the snow, its eyes glazed in terror as the dogs ripped open its bloody flank, laying bare its violet flesh.

She grabbed Tony under the arms, smelling the heat of the dogs and the blood, and pulled him back, dragging him as far as she could away from the dog pack.

Behind a tree, they clung together, shivering. "Cindy, you all right?" he said.

"Yes, let's get away from here."

With one arm around Cindy's neck and using a stick as a crutch, Tony struggled to his feet. Then they hobbled along with what strength they still had, putting as much distance as they could between themselves and the dogs.

19

TWO SOLDIERS

FLEEING THE wild dogs, they had lost everything.

They moved hypnotically, arms around each other, one step at a time. Tony didn't think about being rescued. His whole world had been narrowed down to Cindy. Moving, his arm was always around her shoulder. When they stopped, he didn't let her out of his sight.

They were, at last, past the swamp and the ravine, in hilly country. All afternoon they plodded slowly through the snow, yoked together like a pair of dumb beasts. They were so weak that when they fell in the snow they lay there, unmoving, until they found the strength to help each other up and hobble on again.

Late in the afternoon, on top of an incline, Cindy pitched forward and rolled down the hill like a snowball.

At the bottom she lay motionless. It scared Tony. "Cindy!" He started hopping, stumbled, fell, and rolled the rest of the way to her side. "Cindy, Cindy, you all right?"

She was laughing weakly, tears coming from her eyes. She was covered with snow. He thought she'd finally lost all strength, snapped. She was pointing. "Look, Tony."

At first he couldn't believe his eyes. Picnic tables stacked on end in a long row like a thick fence, and beyond them the green pipe frames of empty swing sets. He rubbed his eyes. It didn't go away. They were in a picnic area with snow-covered stone fireplaces, and in the middle of the cleared area a small, shuttered brown building. The picnic ground was closed for the winter, but there had to be a road. Even if it was unplowed, they had a direction now, a way to follow.

They were so tired and so excited that they drifted around aimlessly until Tony began poking through the garbage cans for scraps. They were ravenous. One garbage can after another was empty and scoured clean. Cindy was quickly discouraged. "One more can," Tony said. "Maybe hunters were here after they closed the picnic grounds." Almost as he spoke he came up with a brown paper bag and in it half a loaf of frozen bread. He divided it carefully.

Gnawing on the bread, they talked about what they would do next. Tony wanted to push on, but he wasn't serious. His ankle pained him, and they were both so exhausted and languid that they could only stagger around together and laugh into each other's shoulders.

They had to rest. They had to get warm. They couldn't go on today.

Together they broke into the brown-shingled building, a men's bath and shower room. A gray concrete floor, three shower stalls, three toilet stalls to the right, three sinks under three small square mirrors to the left. In a mirror Tony saw Cindy, and next to her a wild looking person with dark, gaunt cheeks and hollow black eyes under a tangle of wild, filthy hair.

"That's me," he muttered in astonishment.

"Your own beautiful self," she said.

Tony talked about dragging a picnic table into the men's room to sleep on. They didn't have the strength to do that, either. They were only able to start a fire in the middle of the floor, using rolls of toilet paper and a clump of last fall's dried leaves that had blown into a corner. They slept near the fire on the cold concrete floor, wrapped together. Tony slept heavily at first, then the pain in his ankle brought him awake. Cindy didn't move. Had she stopped breathing? He listened till he heard the steady, regular rhythm of her breath. The shadows of the fire flickered on the ceiling, and he thought of his family.

Then he remembered the snow, the woods they'd come through that day, the dogs, and the blood of the deer. He couldn't have survived without Cindy. They'd lived ten days in the snow, stayed alive by their own efforts and ingenuity. Now he was tired, terribly tired, but filled with hope again and eager for the morning.

It was snowing again as Lillian Littlejohn, who lived

on Old French Road, watched her two children get on the Redfield Central School bus. The bus moved off slowly. Clara Watacky, who was driving, was more cautious than some. Mrs. Littlejohn stood at the window until the bus disappeared around the turn in the road. She was alone now, as she was every day after the children and Neil went off.

There was always this moment when everything stopped, the silence coming down around her shoulders like a mantle. She had work to do, the laundry machines to start, a letter to write to her sister in Syracuse, a cake she'd promised to bake for a church bake sale, and so on. But she enjoyed this moment, the silence and peace. She and Neil had moved to Old French Road two years before, taking over a farmhouse that needed a lot of do-it-yourself work. They liked the space and quiet, and being so close to the state lands. They lived in the very last house on Old French Road, two miles before the entrance to the Roaring Brook State Park. It was a good life, particularly when Neil and the children were home with her.

Mrs. Littlejohn couldn't help worrying about the children when they were away from her. She remembered the pictures she'd seen in the Watertown Times of the children who had been missing for nearly two weeks and still hadn't been found. They were unrelated, one a girl and the other a boy. They didn't come from the same place, but they had disappeared on the same day in roughly the same country, leading to conjecture that their fate was somehow linked. Almost two weeks, Mrs. Littlejohn thought. It must be awful for their parents.

It was still snowing later in the day and the plow hadn't come through. It gave Mrs. Littlejohn some anxious moments. If the snowfall seemed as if it would be unusually heavy, the school would send the children home early on the bus. Winter in this north country wasn't easy. Twice this winter the neighbors down at the four corners had to bring the children home on their snowmobiles.

Later, measuring a chair for a slipcover, she glanced out the window, looking for the school bus, and noticed two strange figures coming slowly into sight, trudging down the unplowed road leading from the state park grounds. Which was strange, to say the least. And the way they looked! For a moment she thought they were two small black bears, they were so rough-looking.

Mrs. Littlejohn was curious, and then uneasy. These days you never knew. People did such peculiar things. She was sorry now they'd not gotten another dog after their old bitch, Sara, had died. The closer the pair came, the odder they seemed. They were both bundled in rags, their faces dark, snow and frost clinging to their clothes and skin. The taller one had his frowsy head wrapped in a scarf, and was leaning on his companion. Mrs. Littlejohn had never seen anything like them. They reminded her of pictures she'd seen of wounded soldiers retreating from a battlefield.

They turned at the foot of the driveway and came slowly toward her house. She hurried to the door and opened it, stepping out front. "Hello?" she called cautiously. "Hello . . . what is it? What do you want?"

20

YES, I KNOW
IT'S A MIRACLE

TONY'S HOSPITAL room was so crowded that there wasn't space for another person to stand, but still they kept coming. His Aunt Irene, his Uncle Mike, and his three cousins were there. His sisters were all sitting on his bed. Flo was writing something on his cast. His mother was sitting by his side, stroking his hand. At the door, his father was shaking hands with people as they came. Uncle Leonard winked at him from the foot of the bed.

There were flowers on the windowsill, and the telephone ringing with calls from relatives in Akron and Chicago, and his father's other brother in St. Petersburg, Florida. "He's all right . . . yes, he's perfect except for his ankle . . . Yes, he lost quite a bit of weight,

but other than that . . . Yes, I know it's a miracle . . .
We thought the worst these last few days. . . ."

Following his mother's whispered directions, Tony
was sitting up for the people, smiling and saying something to everyone. But after a while it was hard for him
to focus. He let his head go back against the pillow and
his mind drift the way it had so often when he and
Cindy were trudging through the deep snows. Part of
him was still there, in that other world.

His Uncle Mike thrust his pale, heavy face close to
Tony's. "Did you see any big animals, Anthony, any
bear or mountain lions?"

"Just dogs, Uncle Mike."

"They must have run for their life when they seen
you coming, Anthony," his uncle said, nudging Tony's
father. "The Laportes would scare the bejesus out of
anybody."

His father laughed. "You don't think there's another boy who could have done what my boy did."

Tony closed his eyes. The sound of the voices in
the background rippled over him. "He's tired . . . poor
kid . . . we better go." He heard his mother saying
goodbye to the people until only his family remained.
He opened his eyes. "Don't go yet."

His mother and father sat down with him. His older
sister remained, but the two younger girls went off to
buy cokes from the machine. Alone with his parents,
Tony felt a little awkward. He wanted to say something
to them about getting into a rage over the dog and
taking the car. "I'm sorry about the car. I really wrecked
it."

"It was an old car," his mother said. "We bought it for seventy-five dollars, so don't worry."

"What about the tires and battery?" his father said. "They cost something."

"Oh, Fred," his mother said.

"I want to pay for it," Tony said. "You tell me how much it costs, and I'll pay it all back."

"How you going to do that, you crazy kid?" his father said. "We're just glad you're alive. So forget about the money and the car. I don't know how you did it, in that weather for eleven days. How'd you keep from freezing?"

Tony shook his head. He'd told them about the fires they'd made and the things they'd done to keep warm, but somehow he never got to say what he wanted to say about what those eleven days had really meant.

The car—he could talk about that. He'd taken the car and wrecked it. Now it was up to him to make it good. They kept saying it didn't matter, that having him home alive and whole was all they cared about. They didn't understand that it did matter to him. When he'd taken the car he'd acted like a spoiled, punk kid. He wanted them to know he wasn't that way anymore, but he didn't know how to say it. He knew Cindy would understand. If she was here, she'd be able to explain it better.

21

THE LETTER

Dear Tony,

 First of all, it was great talking to you on the phone and even greater getting your letter, although you are not much of a letter writer. Let's be honest! "Hello, how are you, I'm fine, my ankle is mending okay . . ." is all right as far as it goes. But it doesn't go very far. I want to hear from you, Tony. I want to know how you are, the real you, the inside you— do you follow me, old fellow? Sure you do.

 The best part of your letter was your saying you'd come visit me. Oh, do, do, do, Tony! I want to see you, I want to talk to you.

 It's all changed, hasn't it? They're the same, but we're not. None of them really understand. They

*think now that we're clean again and they've fed us
and looked us over, poked down our throats, taken
our pulses, weighed and measured us—then it's okay.
We can just go back being the old Tony and
Cindy. But it isn't so.*

*My father wanted to know about you, what kind
of person you are, and how you behaved during the
ordeal. That's what he calls it. Ordeal is right.*

*Wow, it's great to be warm, isn't it? And have
Rice Krispies and toast with butter and a glass of real
orange juice for breakfast. Tony, I've been eating like
a pig all week, but I'll never be as chubby as I was.
And how about sleeping in a real bed with clean
sheets, and taking a hot bath, and changing your
clothes every day? And knowing that people are
happy you're here and keep coming around to look
at you and kiss you and shake their heads. I didn't
know there were that many people who knew I ex-
isted, or cared.*

*We nearly died, Tony. We could have, a num-
ber of times. We did a lot of dumb things, and a lot
of good, smart things. Dad said we saved ourselves.
I'm going to tell you how I feel about that—whether
you want to know or not. (Of course you do, says
Cindy wisely.) Listen, here's the thing. Tony, we
were born once to our mothers, as everyone is. But
this time, we gave birth to ourselves. You know what
I mean. You were there. You are my brother now,
and although you hardly need any more sisters, you're
stuck with me for life.*

I wonder if I'll ever be as happy as I am right

now, as aware of everything. Every day has been so sharp for me, I've never been so aware of the color, the touch, the feel of each moment.

Well, enough of Cindy's blabbing. You come see me, brother. And yes, I'm coming to see you, too. Your mom wrote me a great note, which I'm going to answer next, and invited me to visit over spring holidays. Your little sister sent me a drawing. She sounds like a character I'm going to love. In fact, your whole family will probably end up on my list of all-time favorite people. And I hope my dad and I will stand high on your list.

Lots of love from your fourth sister,

Cindy